THE GENTLEMAN

by Jacob Enns

First Edition – September 2012

ISBN
978-1-4602-0240-1 (Hardcover)
978-1-4602-0241-8 (Paperback)
978-1-4602-0242-5 (eBook)

Published by:

FriesenPress
Suite 300 – 852 Fort Street
Victoria, BC, Canada V8W 1H8

www.friesenpress.com

Distributed to the trade by The Ingram Book Company

Cover design by Tommy Enns

Note:

Names, events, and places in this book are in no way connected or related to any people or places. Similarities of names, events or places are purely coincidental.

Chapter 1

The alarm went off at five o'clock on Saturday morning, waking Jeff Nolan from a deep, but troubled sleep. He, instinctively, reached out to his nightstand and hit the snooze button. It would go off again in five minutes. He felt groggy from work fatigue, but the dream was there again, clear, as it was many mornings when his alarm went off. This morning he was not going in to work. He remained in bed, wishing the dream was the reality and the reality was only a dream.

The alarm would go off again but, for the next little while, his mind had time to think. The week at work had been long. He had decided a few months earlier to go hunting this fall and it had been difficult getting his foreman at work to allow him to take time off, even just for one Saturday. Things were too busy at the trailer factory.

Where Jeff worked, it was the same thing every day. In Western Canada, grain production had increased in recent years and Jeff's employer kept him busy, together with a small group of employees, building grain trailers, putting in ten hour days cutting and welding parts together, and then grinding and polishing the finished trailers to a shine. For over fourteen years now he had been at this work and, some days, he was bored with his job.

At 225 pounds, and 6 foot 6", Jeff was big but in good shape. His broad chest and shoulders made him an imposing figure. Under the heavy physical demands of his work, his body maintained its fitness and muscle strength. It felt good to be healthy and strong. But, since becoming a young widower, his work seemed to have lost much of its meaning. The love of his life had died, and something inside him had been left lonely, empty, cold and numb.

Two years ago, some of his co-workers, in an attempt to help him get over his loss, had insisted that he join them on a hunting trip. They knew, from his past, that he was a good hunter. "It will be good for you," they'd said. Jeff had not been so sure. It seemed to him that nothing much mattered anymore, since he was alone. It was not that he didn't like hunting, or was not familiar with guns. Back in high school, he had always shot his dad's guns out on the farm. He had enjoyed shooting wildlife back then, for varmint control and hunting deer.

When he had gotten married, he shifted his interests more towards camping and hiking with his young wife, Faye. Those were the days when he'd felt like a king. Since Faye's death, it was as if the wind had gone out of the sails of his soul. It was as if his life-ship was stuck in an arctic wilderness of pack ice. He had been through a long grieving process, but still found it hard to face life—it had dealt him a cruel blow, with the death of Faye.

His friends at church had been understanding and had given him space to grieve, and the coworkers had tried to cheer him up. The guys at work had sort of reintroduced him to the sport of hunting, and he'd discovered that he really enjoyed it. In two years, he had gone out hunting with the guys twice.

That first hunting trip had been good and, in a way, it was a healing experience. Hunting somehow reconnected him with his past and his early teenage years again. This morning, when the alarm went off, he had been dreaming of his lovely wife Faye again, and been woken up to another day of dark loneliness.

At the sound of the second alarm, Jeff turned it off and sat up. He shook his head, as if to bring himself to the present again. He got out of bed, went into the kitchen and turned on the coffee maker. By the time he had showered, the coffee would be ready.

Max and Brick, his two Huskies, were still lying by the wood stove, looking as if they were wondering what the early-morning moving around was all about. The dogs had been little puppies when Jeff got them. He had made a trip up north, and met a trapper who had sold them to him for a good price, 400 dollars a piece. Jeff and the dogs were inseparable, when work gave them the option. Every morning when Jeff left the house to go to work, Max and Brick would whine, wishing their master would remain home with them.

Mrs. Paten, a retired school teacher living with her husband a little ways down the gravel road, would come later in the morning and take the dogs for an hour-long walk. Because the dogs needed more than just a walk, she would throw Frisbees and have the dogs chase them for a good while, to tire them out. Then she'd put them in the dog pen behind Jeff's house. There was a large kennel, and an area that was fenced in where the dogs could run and play to their heart's content. In the evening, when Jeff came home, he would bring his dogs in. This time of year, in this part of Alberta, the sun set early, and it was pretty close to being dark by the time he got home.

On this November morning, as Jeff was getting up, his mind was still with Faye. He thought of her every night when he went to sleep, and every morning he got up with her still in his mind. It had been just over four years since she'd died. He remembered it as it if were yesterday. It had been one of those clear, cold, short, crisp winter days when being alive felt good. They had come home from church in the morning and had lunch together. That afternoon, Faye had mentioned she felt a bit fatigued, but suggested that if she went for a walk, it might bring her around. Jeff had wondered why she wanted to go for a walk if she felt fatigued, but agreed and they had gone out. That walk had not lasted long. Behind his property there was a field that belonged to a local farmer and it was on his lane way that Jeff had taken Faye. He would remember that walk forever. It had been his last walk with Faye.

Jeff had married Faye, his high-school sweetheart, when she'd been just barely twenty, and he just twenty one. Their marriage had been a honeymoon for the first several years.

Then they had discovered that Faye couldn't have children. It had been a huge blow for them both. Jeff thought back to the day when the doctor had told them that it would take a miracle, literally, for them to have a child. Medically speaking, it would never happen. Her reproductive organs were not developed properly, but Jeff had decided that the verdict from the doctor would not spoil his love for his wife. Instead, he tried that much harder to show her that he cared and loved her. To him, she was the crown of his life, regardless of what her health was like. Even though she was not able to have children, in his heart she was still the image of perfection. She was a gift from God to him. He had not married Faye for what he could get from her, or what she would do for him. To him, Faye was a beautiful person to love and cherish, to share his life with, and enjoy simply for who she was, not for what her abilities were. And that's what he did for the next seven years, until everything changed forever.

The memory of that sunny winter Sunday in January, four years ago, was etched in Jeff's mind like chiseled ice, carved into his mind. When they had gotten back to the house from their walk, Faye had mentioned that the fatigue was still there, and now in addition to feeling fatigued, she had a tight feeling in her chest. Jeff wanted to take her to town to the emergency. She had brushed it off as nothing that a good cup of hot tea and a rest by the wood stove wouldn't take care of.

The tight feeling persisted. Later that evening it got worse. Jeff decided to take her to the emergency, twenty five kilometres away, in town. On the way to town, he realized that Faye was worse off than he had thought, or that she had admitted. By the time he got her to the emergency room at the small hospital, she was having difficulty breathing. She was rushed into intensive care.

Jeff had called Pastor Raymond Thomson, telling them that he had brought Faye to the hospital in Forest Hill, and she wasn't doing so well. Pastor Thomson and his wife Betty had come that night, and spent some time with Jeff and Faye. It had felt good to feel valued and cared for. Faye had not been doing well, but she had tried to be brave as she struggled with her breathing and pain. The doctors had worked hard trying to find out what was ailing Faye, but they had had difficulty figuring out and pinpointing what was wrong.

Over the next few days, more people from their church community had come to visit, bringing flowers and cards. This had been new to Jeff. He had never been in the hospital in his life, except for a few brief visits when a relative of his had been ill. He had always been healthy and wasn't used to getting this kind of attention. As the days came and went, Faye didn't get better. For several weeks, Faye had clung to life. Tests showed that her body was infected with a rare virus. The doctors tried what they could, but her body didn't respond to treatments.

Faye had slipped away and, in a matter of weeks, she was gone. For Jeff, his world had collapsed around him. It was like it just imploded. Faye had been more than his pride and joy in life, she had been a part of his soul. With her gone, it seemed as though the spark in his life was gone and, with her death, his life's sun had set. An endless icy night, frozen in time, had set in, and that was where he now lived. In his heart he hoped he would some day wake up from this nightmare. But it was not to be.

The funeral had been held in the small, Hope Fellowship Church. It was a simple, white, clapboard-sided church building, where Jeff had gone as a little boy with his father and mother and, later on, in his teen years, he had become a member there. This was the church where he had made his commitment, and his confession, to the faith of his mother and father, and their parents before them. There he had been baptized, and there he had married Faye.

That was four years ago but, this November morning, under the warm shower, Jeff's mind continued wandering back to the past, to how life had been before he'd lost her, as though the water from the warm shower had helped thaw out and ease the pain from the frozen memories.

It had been a deep loss to him when his parents died, but he had told himself that that was the cycle of life. When Faye had died, even though there were some similarities to the deaths of his parents, it had still been very different. There were no words with which he could comfort himself now, no way to justify the loss. With the death of his mother and father, there too was a sense loss and grief, but also of celebration, of completion. His parents had had lived well, and had finished their course in life. Faye's death was like a race cut short. When she died, then too their friends and families had come together and grieved with him over the loss of his wife. But nothing eased the pain. There was nothing to celebrate.

Jeff and Faye had had a lot of friends back then. But, after the funeral, he had withdrawn into himself. At first, people from church had brought food, and spent time with him, trying to bring him comfort, but it didn't seem to bring any warmth to the dark, icy pain and despair. He had become a recluse. Life was not fair. He figured he had loved his dear Faye as well as any man could love a woman. Why had she been taken from him? Had he perhaps not been good enough for her? No. That couldn't be. He had loved her with all of his heart and more. But why had she been taken? That was, and remained, an unanswered question.

Their marriage had lasted only 10 short years and, in those years of marriage, Jeff and Faye had always wanted to have children. Because they could not have their own biological children, they had several times talked of adoption, but each time they had backed off. It was Jeff who'd decided against adoption. He couldn't reconcile himself to the fact of raising someone else's child. Now he regretted that he had not shown more interest in adopting a child, for his own sake as well as for Faye. Now, with Faye gone, he sometimes wished for human companionship. In his mind, he felt someone had failed him. But how was he to express it? Who would listen without judging him? He had been taught that God was good, and if that was the case, the problem must be his.

Jeff had made a decision some time after Faye's death, that he would continue on with life, regardless of what cards he'd been dealt. But nothing eased the loneliness, or brought warmth to his heart. He had started to go to church again on Sunday mornings, but kept to himself. Most of the people he and Faye had hung out with were moving on with their lives, but it seemed he could not forget Faye. She had been the light of his life. While the other couples were raising their children, some of them now in their teens, it seemed to Jeff that his life just remained frozen solid in time. It seemed that the couples he and Faye had hung out with were enjoying life. He wanted to get his life back on track. Today he was going hunting.

Chapter 2

Jeff's mind came back to the present as he turned off the shower. This November morning was the first time Jeff was going hunting by himself. Max and Brick, his two healthy huskies, were coming with him, but no other person. He had trained them to carry saddle bags, and pull sleds. He figured that once he shot and dressed his deer; the dogs would help him carry the meat back to his truck. They could each easily carry some good sized pieces of venison. He got dressed and went over to the cupboard, took out a cup and poured himself a steaming cup of coffee.

Before he sat down to sip his coffee and eat his toast, he reached to the shelf and took out a can of dog chow, opened it and dumped the canned meat into the dog dish for Max and Brick. This was their morning ritual, only today it was two hours earlier. They needed this early starting time because they had a few hours drive up north, to Beaver's Creek where Jeff hoped to bag his deer.

It was as if Max and Brick knew something was up this morning. Eagerly, they gulped down their dish of meat chunks, and then looked up at their master, expectantly. Jeff looked into the eyes of both dogs, and felt a sense of pride. These dogs were animals, but, to him, they were more. They had become like family to him.

Jeff sipped his coffee, and finished his toast. He got up from the table, and walked over to the closet where he kept his hunting and camping gear. He hoped to be gone not more than 36 hours. Sunday evening, tomorrow, he hoped to be back home again. He got his Remington 30-06 rifle, a box of shells, and his 'hunting bag'. Inside it, he kept a compass, matches, a rope, a fold-up shovel, a blanket, some cloth to wrap meat in, a few sharp knives, a set of lightweight aluminum camping dishes and some first aid equipment.

The one knife was special. It had a heavy, 12 inch blade–strong enough to use as a machete, almost as a small axe if he ever needed one. It had a nice leather sheath. As an afterthought, he took the large hunting knife, and put it inside the sheath of his heavy winter boot. Next, he put on his heavy, insulated, camouflage pants, his fleece-lined camouflage hunting coat, and his fur hat. In his coat, he kept a lighter and a Leatherman multipurpose tool.

It was cold outside this morning, almost freezing, but with his winter clothing he would be well protected. He grabbed his rolled-up sleeping bag, reached into the closet and got out the two saddle bags for his dogs. He held them up for his dogs to see.

"You'll be wearing these by this evening, hopefully," Jeff said to his dogs. "And they'll be full of venison. How about that?"

With the cold November air, there would be no danger of the meat spoiling. In fact, overnight it might even freeze unless he kept the saddle bags strapped to the dogs, or close to a campfire—that was, if he should be overnight in the bush. In his mind, Jeff could see the dogs drooling over choice chunks of meat around a campfire that evening. It was going to be a good hunting trip.

It was as if the dogs understood. Both dogs looked at Jeff with eyes of expectation, and ears pointed forward. These dogs were not very large animals, but they were strong. For a fleeting moment Jeff wondered what would happen if ever they became angry, and turned on him. Quickly he brushed the thought aside, confident that with him being their gentle master his dogs were perhaps the most loyal friends he would ever have.

Jeff reached into the pantry, took four cans of dog food from the shelf, and stuffed them into a small backpack. 'You'll need these for tonight and tomorrow, and maybe a few extra if we don't get any meat, and are not back by tomorrow,' Jeff spoke, more to himself than anyone else in particular. Next, he took two cans of corned beef, some canned corn and two bags of trail mix, and threw them in too, along with some beef jerky. He reached into the fridge and took out some small water bottles.

"This will do till we get back, boys,' Jeff spoke again to his dogs. "Let's go." He stuffed the food, the sleeping bag, his hunting bag, and the saddle bags, into a large backpack, and then slung it over his shoulders. He picked up his rifle and headed toward the door, the dogs at his heels.

Outside, the wind was fairly brisk, coming from the west. Being November, it was a cold wind. Jeff didn't have an attached garage to his house. He kept his truck outside, by a small workshop in which he sometimes tinkered with some hobby manufacturing. Even though it was only about 60 feet from his small bungalow to his shop, the wind had a bite, and it chilled his face. It was still pitch-black outside, and he could not see the stars. It was overcast and it felt like it might snow at any time. Jeff carried his gear to his 2001, four-door dodge pickup. He opened the back door and the dogs jumped in. This was not the first time he had taken them on a trip.

Jeff reached into his backpack and, in the light of the cab, double-checked that he had everything. It was all there. He put the pack on the floor between the seats.

With both dogs inside, and his gear in the back, Jeff walked to the front of the truck, and unplugged the block heater. Even though it was not very cold yet, he plugged his truck in early in the Fall, when the frost began. He got in behind the wheel and started the truck. He let it run for a few seconds, to let the engine settle into a steady smooth idle. Then he put the gear lever in reverse and backed away from his workshop, with the gravel crunching under the tires as he made the turn. He put the truck into drive and began driving out of his long gravel driveway. He reached over and turned the heater dial to full heat, and the fan to medium, and directed the air to defrost. He didn't want his windshield to fog up. At the end of his driveway he turned right, heading north. It would be a few hours drive before he got to where he'd start walking.

The two previous years, when he'd gone with his buddies from work, they had gone farther west, and had been gone for a few days. But they'd also not been quite so busy at the shop at that time either. Jeff wanted to go by himself this year, and stay closer to home. He needed time by himself, away from everything. A neighbour of his had gotten a good sized buck by Beaver's Creek, about 200 or so kilometres north. The land there was rolling, and more wooded. There was just nothing out there, but miles and miles of hills, trees and rocks. He looked forward to a full day of solitude, maybe two.

Jeff guided his pickup north, up 35 toward Beaver's Creek. He hoped the road would be good. It was gravel, and leading toward some logging camps in the far north. This time of year there was little or no traffic. Traffic would start up in the dead of winter when the roads were frozen. The ground was still too soft. They would have to wait for some time of hard frost before they could start hauling logs.

The road was not well traveled most of the year, and not the best maintained. As he continued driving through the early morning, Jeff kept his eyes peeled, watching the road, which was illuminated by the truck's headlights. In this area, one could never know what to expect. He drove for a while, and let his mind wander. The 4x4 pickup had a V8 engine under the hood that kept up a steady rumble as he guided the truck through the morning darkness. He had filled his tank the night before, on his way home from work, and was good for at least 600 kilometres of travel.

After a while, Jeff started getting bored. He switched on the cab light, and took a quick glance into the back of the cab. He could see that the dogs were lying contently on the back seat, dozing off. He turned the light off again. He turned on the radio. Out this far north, he was beyond clear good reception of the FM frequency reach of any station. He turned to the AM settings and got CMNB. Some country song was playing, and Jeff was about to turn it off when the news announcer interrupted the song and came on the air.

"Good morning, everyone out in North Country. It is seven o'clock and here is the news for this early November morning."

Jeff was surprised at how long he had been driving already, and decided not to turn off the radio. As he kept driving, what he heard caused his heart to skip a beat. It was that story again. The one he'd been so shocked by when he'd read about it yesterday. The announcer was talking about the disappearance of a woman, named Eileen Benson.

He remembered the news of the previous night. He had gone into Forest Hill for some groceries, and had seen the local paper on the news-stand. The headline had caught his attention. "MISSING WOMAN". Her name was Eileen Benson, a 27-year-old real estate agent, with blonde hair, and blue eyes, and 5'4". According to one source, Eileen had mentioned to a friend that she had to show a house to a potential buyer out by Pond Mill road, about 12 kilometres east of Forest Hill. She'd said she would be back later in the evening, but had not returned.

When Eileen still had not returned the next morning, her friend Ruby had notified the police. She'd been told that they wouldn't begin a search until she'd been missing for 24 hours. Her friend Ruby had decided to wait and see if Eileen had returned when she got home from work in the evening. When there was still no sign of her that evening, Ruby had sensed that something was wrong and had decided to drive to the Real Estate property on her own to see if she could find Eileen. She had found the property just as Eileen had described it, a brick ranch house with an attached garage, on a three-acre parcel of land. There was a "for sale" sign by the road.

What Ruby had found strange was that Eileen's Ford focus was parked in the driveway. This was not normal. She again called the police. "Eileen would have called," Ruby had said to the police. She had been sure of that. Something was strange, given that Eileen's car was there, but there was no sign of her. Ruby had not dared go onto the actual property. She just drove by and reported what she saw.

The police began to investigate and, that evening, the story aired on the radio. The police had gone to the house on Mill Pond road and made an investigation. The car was there, but it was unlocked, and it looked as if everything was in place. Nothing seemed to be missing. They had found the front door closed but also unlocked. When the police had gone inside, they had found an alarming scene. There were clear signs of

a struggle. They had found some blood stains on the floor, and some curtains ripped off the windows, and missing. Something had definitely happened in that house.

Now, on the radio Jeff was listening to, was an update of that story. A few days had passed, and there was still no sign of her anywhere, and no phone calls either. No one had seen anybody, or anything, suspicious. The only thing that had been mentioned was that someone had seen a blue GMC safari van at the grocery store, and that the van seemed kind of odd. That van was not one from around the area. Other than that there was nothing.

The announcer's next phrase jolted Jeff back to the present. "If you have seen any suspicious activity, or strange persons, or vehicles, you are asked to contact the police." The announcer gave the phone number to contact. Jeff instinctively reached to his waist, where he always kept his cell phone. It was there. He wore his cell phone like it was part of him. He would not leave home without it. "As far as running into a missing woman" Jeff thought, "or a kidnapper, well, what are the chances of that?" He focused back on going deer hunting, and on his own life. The radio went to a commercial break and Jeff turned it off.

His mind went back again to the early years of his marriage to Faye, and before that. When he started dating her, he realized her love and zest for life. Her dreams had been to be a mother and to work in horticulture. She loved everything that had to do with life. She loved animals and plants, and never seemed to tire of hiking and camping. She said that it brought her close to nature. She got her wish to work with plants and animals, but had not been privileged to be a mother. Jeff's mind wandered. "What wouldn't I give to have my sweetheart back?" he thought.

The truck continued northward. After what seemed like a long time of driving on County Road 35, Jeff turned the truck down a narrow, even less-travelled, gravel road heading to the northwest. He followed the description his neighbour had given him of the road. It was still dark, but the sky to the east was beginning to show signs of the coming day. It would be getting light soon. The winding road here was not as good as 35 had been.

After another few kilometres, the road ended and gave him the option of turning left or right. He turned to the right, heading north again. As he turned, Jeff noticed that it almost looked as though there was a set of tire tracks leading to the left. "Well," he thought, "so what if it is. Perhaps it's just another hunter doing what I'm doing."

He was getting close the place where he'd park his truck. From there, he'd head out on foot for another few kilometres or so. His intention was not to drive down directly to Beaver's Creek. By taking the right, he would be on the east side of Beaver's Creek. He figured that since the wind was coming out of the west, he would walk to Beaver's Creek from the east with the wind in his face. There was a hill he would have to make his way over, but it was not a steep climb, at least from what his neighbour had described to him. Going in this way against the wind there would be less chance of his scent scaring away any deer away that might be there.

Jeff drove a short distance more, and pulled off the narrow road toward the left, parking the truck among some trees, somewhat hidden from sight. There were light tracks made by his truck, but the ground was hard, and no one would easily spot his brown pickup behind the thick undergrowth.

It took Jeff only a few minutes to get his dogs and his gear out of the truck. He took the compass out of his hunting bag and, even though he could tell which way was west in the early morning, by the direction of the wind as it was still blowing, he looked at his compass and got his bearings. "West is that way, boys," he said to his dogs. They were eager for this walk.

After walking for about 15 minutes up an incline, Jeff knew he was getting closer to Beavers' creek. According to the description given him, it was over the next knoll, and then down maybe a kilometre or so more. The wind was still brisk here, coming down the knoll, and toward him. It was quite cold, but he was well dressed. Jeff wondered what the thermometer reading would be. It was not quite daylight yet, but by now he could clearly see the terrain and his surroundings.

He kept walking. About 50 yards from the top of the knoll, Max stopped all of a sudden, and perked his ears. Jeff noticed it immediately. He stopped, not making a sound. In a low voice, he spoke to Max. "What is it?" The dog just stood there, his ears pointed forward, and jaws closed tight. He let out a very low, almost whispered growl. Jeff hunched down beside his dog. "Come on Max, what is it? Is something wrong?" Brick, seemed to notice something too, but was not quite as alert.

Jeff paused, wondering. "What if there's something other than a deer up ahead?" He waited a few moments. He slid his 30-06 off his back and put it to his shoulder, taking off the scope shields. He peered through the scope and scanned the area up ahead of him, but he could see nothing—just trees, grass and rocks.

It was a good thing the wind, at least, was in his favour. Whatever it was that was up ahead, would not hear him or smell him—if he kept a low profile and kept quiet. The trees were not very dense here. It would be fairly easy to spot a moving object if someone or something was on the lookout for it. Jeff knew he would have to be careful. If whatever was making noise was a deer, he could shoot it, dress it and be back home early, almost too early. He had mentally prepared himself to have at least a full day out here by himself with his dogs. But he had a sense of foreboding about this. His heart began beating fast. He looked down again at Max. He knew the dog had picked up something that was not normal. For some reason, he had misgivings about the dog's behaviour. Jeff decided not to take chances at being heard or seen. He moved very slowly, carefully placing his steps and making sure he would not step on anything that could snap or make a loud noise. He stopped again and waited several minutes more.

"Okay, boys," Jeff said quietly to his dogs, "whatever is over that knoll, let's go and take a look." The dogs had been well trained to be quiet, and to stay put when told. Slowly and carefully Jeff walked on, up to the knoll and looked down the hill through the trees. He could see nothing. He was still walking against the wind. Even though the wind was not strong, it was enough to make hearing a bit difficult. "Let's keep moving boys,' Jeff whispered to his dogs.

Steady, with measured steps, Jeff walked down the hill toward the valley below. This was the area called Beaver's creek. This was the general area where his neighbour had gotten his buck last year. Jeff was hoping to get his this year, but right now he was not feeling very safe. Something was wrong. The dogs were not behaving normally.

After walking for about another 100 yards, Jeff stopped. Max and Brick stood still too, their ears pointed forward. Jeff listened. He could hear nothing but the noise of the wind in the sparse trees and the grass. Jeff turned to his dogs and spoke in a hushed tone. "Slowly boys, and very quiet." Jeff continued walking. He kept his rifle in his hand now, ready to raise and shoot. If it was a bear, he wanted to be ready. His dogs followed quietly.

Since he had left his truck, with the time it took walking up and over the hill, the morning light had come to the terrain, and through the trees Jeff could now see more of the surroundings. No doubt the creek below would have free-running water, and shade trees, making it a perfect place for deer to come for shelter from the elements, as well as to drink. And with deer present, predators could be present too. It was only a matter of time and he would see the bottom of the valley. Suddenly Max stood still, and again let out that low-whispered growl. This time, Jeff sensed the dog tense up beside him. He crouched down beside his dog. "What is it Max?" he whispered again, puzzled at the dog's strange behaviour. Jeff decided he would just have to take it slowly and carefully. He would take his time. He was glad he was warmly dressed.

Twenty metres ahead of him, and to the right, there was a huge boulder. Jeff decided to make it to that boulder and wait. Slowly, he moved over to the rock. It was about five feet tall and eight feet in diameter, and protruded from the ground. It gave two things, perfect shelter from the wind, and a good vantage point to look farther down into the valley.

Jeff waited. In reality, only a few minutes went by but, after what seemed like a long time, he heard it. A faint human voice, almost a scream, was carried to them in the wind. Immediately, the dogs jerked to attention. "Quiet," Jack whispered. The wind was still blowing in Jeff's favour, but he was taking no chances.

The noise faded away again. Jeff, now fully certain that something was out there, became nervous. Whatever had made that noise was not a bear, or a deer. He was determined to find out what was down there. He looked through the scope on his rifle, slowly scanning the terrain through the trees. He could see nothing, but he knew he had heard a human voice. "Okay boys," Jeff quietly said to his dogs, "we're going closer. We have to see what this is. If there's a person in trouble, we got to help him, or her." It had been a good a while or more since he had crouched down behind the rock. Jeff moved around the rock and began walking downhill again. He wondered how far it would be to the valley.

He kept his eyes peeled for anything that might look out of the ordinary in a wooded place. After a while of slow walking, he came to some dense underbrush. Just up ahead of that there were some more rocky outcroppings. He figured that if he could get himself onto one of those he might be able to get a better view.

Obediently, his dogs followed silently behind him. He moved silently over to the rocks and, and climbed up. He lay flat on his stomach, and whispered to his dogs to be quiet. He raised his rifle to his shoulder and looked through the scope, over the ledge. There, some distance away in a small clearing, was a blue van. He steadied his scope to get a sharp focus. He could not read the license plate. It was outside of his view. But he could clearly make out the letters on the side of the van—GMC Safari. "That must be the van!" It was all coming together now. "That must be the missing woman! That's where the sound came from!"

Jeff's mind was whirling at top speed now. What should he do? What could he do? He slid down the rocky outcrop and sat there, his heart pounding, his breathing coming fast. "Oh, yeah, yeah, call police." He reached for his cell phone, grabbing it and flipping it open. He dialled 911. He put the phone to his ear. Nothing. He looked at the phone. No bars. "Man! No Signal!!" he thought, "Now what?"

He motioned to his dogs to come close, and with his finger to his lips motioned them to be real quiet. As if they understood, they both squatted down on all fours and inched closer till they were almost touching Jeff.

That van was where the scream had come from. He was sure of it. It was a human voice. It had to be. Jeff shook his head, as if trying to shake his thoughts into some sort of sensibility.

Jeff was thinking. "If this is the blue van that was in town, and if the voice came from a woman ... if it was Eileen Benson who screamed, that means I've stumbled onto a crime scene." Jeff could hardly control the thoughts swirling through his brain. "This is not what I planned," Jeff thought desperately. "Why did I go hunting here? I should have never come here. Now what? I could just turn around and leave this place and no one would ever know I was here. But no, I can't do that. That would be wrong. Someone is in trouble and needs me." Jeff knew in his mind what he had to do, and was going to do. He would not leave this scene without first seeing if he could be of help to the person or persons who needed him.

Jeff motioned the dogs to remain on the ground. He slowly got up behind the rocky outcropping and raised his rifle over it, peering through the scope. Perhaps if he studied the situation for a bit he could get some information. The van was an older model Safari with all-wheel drive. Its tires were knobby winter tires designed for off-road travel. The side and rear windows in the van were closed off with curtains. The passenger and driver side windows were clear. It was obvious that the van had seen better days. Jeff still was not sure if the voice had come from inside the van, or outside somewhere. He was very curious, but he had to be sure of his surroundings before he made a move of any kind.

"Some deer hunting trip this is turning out to be." Jeff muttered to himself as his thoughts settled down a bit. "That van must have been at the house Eileen Benson showed to a client. And that man or men must have kidnapped her." Jeff's mind was trying to put pieces of the puzzle together.

Then the scream came again. This time Jeff could make out the words. "Help Meeee!" Jeff knew unmistakably that it was the voice of a woman, and that it was coming from that direction. The dogs were up instantly at the sound of the scream.

Jeff jerked his head downward to the dogs, and sternly pointed at them. "Down. Quiet." Again, they obeyed.

Jeff was scared now. But he was also angry. He raised himself, stood straight up, and made a decision. He looked down at his dogs and spoke, pointing at them. "Listen here boys, you lie down here, and stay until I come back for you, or call you, do you hear?" The dogs lay down side by side, with an ever-so-faint whimper. "I will get you or call you, okay?" The dogs obeyed. Jeff had no idea what he was going to face. But he could not walk away from this. As a young boy, his father had drilled into him never to turn away from a person in need, regardless of who or what they were. The teaching and training of his parents, kicked in. He resolved in his mind not to abandon this poor soul crying for help. He had to do something, and at the same time he didn't want to risk his dogs getting hurt.

He began walking to the van. He had no way of knowing who or what he would meet, but walking away from this scene was not an option for him. There was no sound coming from the van now. As he walked closer to the van, he lost sight of it because of the trees and brush. On top of the rock he had been able to see it, in a clearing. He made for the general direction of that clearing.

Every so often he would stop to listen for any noise. It was quiet. He came close to the clearing. Again, he paused. He looked, and listened—nothing. He stepped into the clearing and cautiously approached the van. His dogs were up the hill where he had come from, well within calling distance. Jeff kept his rifle at his side, but with the safety on. He had no intention of using it on anyone. He was not sure what to make of this situation. He had never been in this kind of situation before. He wondered what he would do if he was faced with the decision of actually confronting a violent criminal. What if he faced a decision of either having to shoot at another human being, or get shot at himself? He was a pacifist, a man who believed in not resisting an evil person. Even as a hunter, he believed all of life was sacred and deserved respect.

Jeff never killed animals for fun or entertainment. It was always either to get food, or control pests. All human life deserved protection and that was part of the reason he knew he had to do what he could to help this person who had cried for help.

As he walked closer to the van, a wave of fear swept over him, as he realized that he might face the real possibility of getting killed if he interfered with a crime in progress. He was also suddenly very much aware that he might be able to stop a crime, if he was willing to use force. But he had been brought up to believe that taking a human life, or even hurting people, was wrong. In fact, Preacher Thompson had preached many times about loving one's enemies and blessing those who spitefully use others. He had often heard Preacher Thompson point out that Jesus preached a life of non-violence and peace. It was also something his mother and father had taught him and that they themselves had lived by all their lives. They had done a good job of drilling this lesson into him as a young boy.

Jeff clearly remembered the many Sunday school lessons as a child, in which he had learned that violence begets violence. In his younger days, as a lad on the farm, it had never really been a big question to him.

Slowly, Jeff walked closer to the van, thinking all the while about what the person, either inside or near the van, must be going through to utter such a cry for help, and at the same time continuing to wonder how he would handle the situation if it got violent. Would he use force if it came to it? People at work had challenged him on his "Do not kill" beliefs more than once. Would he go to war if need be? He had always told everyone that it was better to love than to hate. And for that reason he could never hurt another human being. He had always believed that he could never hurt another human being, no matter what the circumstances, much less kill one. But now, he was not sure how he would react in this situation. The cry sounded like it came from a female. Would he defend her? He would try to rescue her, that he was sure of. His mind battled intensely, as he considered what type of situation he might face. He thought that perhaps he could rescue this person and no one would have to get hurt.

Jeff approached the van. It looked isolated, as if there was no one around. He was coming up to it from the passenger side. The van was facing north, and the passenger side sliding door was on his side. He stopped several feet away from the van and listened. There was nothing, no sound. He stepped up to the van with his backpack on his shoulder and, with his right hand still holding his rifle, he gripped the sliding door's handle with his left, and slid the door back.

At first glance, it was kind of dark inside the van. The closed curtains and early morning light did little to illuminate the dark interior. It took a moment for his eyes to get adjusted to the limited light in the back. He peered into the van and, when his eyes adjusted he saw a terrifying sight.

He saw her. She was sitting in the back of the van, with her hands behind her back, tied to something on the inside wall of the van, and her ankles fastened to a chain. Her face held a fearful expression. The moment he opened the door and saw her, she startled like a scared rabbit. Quickly, she realized that the man opening the door was a different person than the one she had expected. Her look was one of fear and desperation. Her hair was all messed up and her face was stricken with fear. Her sweater and pants were stained with blood.

The instant she realized it was a different person, she regained her senses. "Please, help me!" the woman pleaded. She was sitting on the floor of the van on some old piece of rug with a light winter coat on her body.

"Who are you, and what are you doing here?" Jeff heard himself saying, not yet fully grasping the significance of what he was facing.

The woman spoke with chattering teeth and at a fast pace, with short sentences that didn't hang together. "My name is Eileen Benson. I'm a real-estate agent. Please, help me. Several days ago I got a call to do a showing to this ... man ... he called himself Bob, but I don't think that's the man's real name. I agreed to show him the house, and I met him at the house he wanted me to show him, and he kidnapped me. He's had me tied up for the last few days. I'm scared, cold and hungry. Please get me out of here."

For a moment, Jeff was too surprised to think logically. His mind was trying to make sense of what he was seeing, and at the same time listening to this woman as she focused on him, as if talking to him would make him have pity on her and help her.

The woman continued randomly at a fast chattering pace. "He allows me a few free minutes several times a day, but he keeps his gun on me when I'm not tied up. He says he will kill me after he is done with me." Jeff's eyes had gotten used to the semi-dark space in the van and he saw her more clearly. She was shivering from both cold and fear.

Jeff realized he would have to act fast. He quickly looked around. He was still standing outside the van. He would have to get inside the van to get the woman free. Given the state of her physical health, he would have to, quite possibly, carry her. His mind raced. What if her kidnapper was watching from somewhere close? Jeff would have to take his chances.

He brushed his thoughts about himself aside and planned his next move. He was not going to abandon this poor human soul. Regardless of his personal risk, he would do his best to help her and get her to safety.

"Here, let me quickly help you get free, and then I will get you to safety. I have a truck just over the hill, over there," Jeff heard himself saying, as he nodded in the direction of his truck. He got inside the van, leaned his rifle against the side of the van, took off his back pack and checked to see how Eileen was tied up. She had been tied with some cotton rope. The way it was tied, there was no way she could have ever freed herself given the condition she was in. Jeff took his knife out, to cut the ropes that bound her hands. He quickly cut through them. Then he focused on the chain around her ankles. The chain was fastened with some mechanics wire. He saw that he would have to cut the wires. He decided he would do this with the wire cutter on his Leatherman tool, to free her and get her out of there. He sized up the situation and then spoke quickly to her. "Miss Benson—"

"No", she interrupted, "just Eileen."

Jeff got ready to work on cutting the wire, examining it closely. He wanted to take all necessary precautions. The way Eileen looked; she was in very poor shape. "Okay, Eileen, I will get you out of here. Listen carefully. I will ask you a few questions while I work on cutting this wire, and answer what you can. Where is this man now?"

"I have no idea. He has been gone for quite some time. I don't have any way to track time, and he just comes and goes as he pleases. He will leave for a long time and then suddenly come back with no warning."

"When do you think he may be back?"

Eileen's voice was very agitated. "Again, I don't know, please just hurry. I think he will be back soon!"

"Okay, Okay," Jeff responded. "Do you know if he has the keys for this van with him? We could just take off in it. On second thought, maybe that's not a good idea. If needs be, I can carry you up the hill and down the other side to my truck, and I can bring you to town. It would be several hours of driving for sure."

"Please Mr. ..."

"Jeff Nolan, my name is Jeff Nolan," Jeff responded.

She was getting increasingly agitated and desperate. "Please Mr. Nolan, hurry. I think he is down by the creek. It is a ways down from here. He has been gone for a while. I think he may have a shelter there, and I know he goes there to get water. Anyway, that's what he has been doing since we got here. Sometimes he stays away quite a while. I know he told me to be quiet. This morning is the first time I screamed. When he gets back and knows I screamed, he will be mad. He is very violent and told me that if I screamed, I would pay for it with pain. He has also told me that he will kill me when he is ready and that I was not his first victim and will not be his last. I don't know where he keeps his keys ... in his pocket I think. Please, get me out of here!" Her teeth chattered as she spoke.

"Here," Jeff said, "let me cut this wire on this chain and I will get you on my back and carry you. Jeff reached for his Leatherman tool in his coat pocket, hoping it would be strong enough to cut through the wires that held the chain to her ankle. Once he got the chain off, he could carry her. As he reached into his pocket, Jeff heard a sound, a very familiar sound, that sent chills up his spine. He heard the click of a shotgun choke being pulled back, as it loaded a shell into the chamber.

Chapter 3

Jeff had heard the click of a shotgun loading a shell into the chamber countless times as a young boy, when he went with his dad on duck hunting trips. Then, he had liked the sound. This time it made his hair stand on end. He whirled around in his crouching position near Eileen, looked up, and then froze with fear. He was looking directly at the muzzle of a 12 gauge shotgun.

"Hold it there Mister, if you want to live." The man standing a few feet from the van had a menacing look of rage on his face. Presently he spoke again: "I got you in my line of fire, and this distance I can't miss. With one shot I will drop you if you make so much as a move. I don't miss. One move and you are dead."

Jeff believed the man's words. This man didn't look like he was joking. It was true what Eileen had said. The man had been away from the van for whatever reasons, one of which obviously was to fetch water. He had a plastic gallon jug of water standing beside him on the ground. A few moments passed with the men staring at each other, but neither saying a word.

Jeff's frozen fear was quickly beginning to give way to anger. He had never wanted to kill a human being in his life. But somehow, he had an urge to get his hands on this man and, at least, immobilize him, in whatever way necessary. The man was rather small, maybe 5 foot 5 inches at the most and no more than 170 pounds. Even though he didn't look very strong, one could never tell. Jeff needed to figure out a way to buy time.

"What do you want?" Jeff asked.

The evil faced man responded with a sharp snarl. "It seems to me that I should be asking you that question. What do you want? And what are you doing in my van? Who gave you permission to go trespassing on my property? In this part of the country I do as I please, and anyone causing interference dies. Do you understand that?" The man's voice rose to a high-pitched yell as he finished his sentence.

Jeff had the sickening, sinking feeling that this man would lose self-control and just randomly fire on him without warning. His life really was in danger.

"Look," Jeff said quickly, "I don't know what is happening. I went deer hunting this morning, and this is the area where I decided to hunt. I came up the other side of this hill and down toward the creek below here. I heard the sound of a voice and this is where it took me. I heard a voice pleading for help, and I just responded to her call. I found her here, and tried to help her."

The evil face of the man broke into a perverse grin. "Oh, she did scream, did she? I told her that if she screamed she would pay for it with pain. I specialize in creating pain. In this part of the country I am my own boss and no one tells me what to do. And no one gets in my way. Here everyone does as

I say, do you hear? EVERYONE DOES AS I SAY." He spoke in a loud and angry tone of bullish authority and power. It was all too clear to Jeff what had happened. The direction of the wind had carried the sound to him, but had prevented it from going downhill toward the stream where the man had spent his time. If only Jeff had been several minutes earlier, he would have made off with the woman. Now he was caught.

Jeff didn't dare turn his head toward Eileen behind him, to see how she was making out. Hopefully she would have enough sense to at least keep her hands behind her back and pretend she was still bound. "Who knows what this maniac would do if he finds out I cut her ropes?" Jeff thought.

"What's your name?" Jeff asked trying to sound calm and self-confident. He didn't want to let on that, inside, he was filled with fear.

"My name? Oh, has she not told you yet? My name is Bob. If I trusted you, I would shake hands with you." He had that devilish grin again. "But as you see, I can't begin trusting my prey, now can I?" He finished, with a sly, drawn out smile.

"What do you want with her?" Jeff asked sharply. In spite of his fear, he was getting angrier and more riled by the moment. The words had barely left Jeff's mouth when the man tightened his grip on his 12 gauge, and it looked as if he might pull the trigger any moment.

"Look here, you fool," he growled. "You don't know me yet. But you will before you die. Both of you are going to die, when I decide you have lived long enough." Then, as if making a quick mental decision, the man gestured toward Jeff with the barrel of his gun.

"You, get down on the floor of the van, *NOW* ... and put your hands behind your back." Jeff hesitated. Bob came closer, his gun aimed at Jeff.

Jeff turned part way, eyeing his rifle leaning against the opposite wall, inside the van. He didn't want to kill anyone, but if he could just even the playing field, and perhaps scare this evil brute, he might get a chance to escape. The 30-06 was within reach of his long arm, but he decided against trying anything. It was just too unsure and risky. It was better to go along with this madman for now, rather than risk getting killed. Jeff instinctively knew that the man was going to tie him up, but there was nothing he could do at this point. So he went down on the floor of the van, face down, and he put his hands behind his back, hoping that somehow he would be able to escape not with just *his* life, but also the life of this kidnapped woman.

"Don't move," the kidnapper barked at him, "or I will put a slug in your head." Jeff was desperately hoping for a window of opportunity, when the man would put away his gun, if only for a brief moment before he got tied up. He was hoping to get a fighting chance, but before the thought was even completed, Jeff felt something blunt on the side of his head, and he blacked out.

Jeff didn't know how long he had been out, but the sound of a motor starting roused him and in an instant he was wide awake. The van! It had started up. His head hurt badly where he had been hit by something. Luckily, he couldn't feel any bleeding. He found himself sitting in the van with his back against the passenger-side wall, near the back fender, almost opposite the woman. He tried to grab hold of a side support from his sitting position, and found he had been tied to a part of the van. He felt something pinching his feet. He looked down and saw the rope. While he had been out, Bob had tied him up, making sure he would not go anywhere.

Jeff glanced to the front. Bob had started the van. The engine was idling and Bob was walking around outside, making sure he was not leaving anything behind. Jeff saw that his hunting pack was lying on the floor of the van, with some of the contents scattered about. A few bottles of water, and some cans of food, had been tossed into a corner. Jeff looked at the woman. She was out, her head hanging limply forward and to one side. She was still sitting where he'd first found her. The left side of her face was swelling up from a beating. Bob had made good on his threat to make her suffer for screaming.

Jeff frantically searched his mind – what to do now? His 30-06 rifle was lying on the floor close to the front. Then he remembered his dogs, Brick and Max. He must find a way to do something! At that moment, Bob opened the driver side door and got behind the wheel, putting the van in gear. Jeff's dogs were still out there, waiting for him to come to them, or call them. Instinctively, Jeff yelled out at the top of his lungs "Max! Brick!"

Bob jerked his head around and glared. "What is that? Who are you yelling for? Is there someone else besides you here? There better not be or you will die right away." Then, just as suddenly, he stepped on the gas and the van moved forward. "We are getting out of here."

Jeff thought quickly. Making that call for his dogs was a mistake. He didn't want this maniac to stop, get his gun and shoot the dogs. Jeff pretended to lose consciousness and slumped forward again, hoping Bob would think he was confused and disoriented from the beating, and blacking out. He was hoping his dogs had heard him. But what chance would his dogs stand against an evil man with a shotgun, and his own rifle at his disposal? This clearly was a man who had no regard for human life, perhaps much less for animals.

The van lurched forward over the rough terrain and down the hill, toward a narrow road. Out of the corner of his eye, Jeff made a mental note of where the van got onto the road.

He would have to remember this place. Off to the right of the road there were a few big pine trees and a large boulder. Jeff decided to think of that place as "Twin pines rock," when he came back ... if he came back. If his dogs didn't follow him, this would be the place he would look for them.

The van got to the road, and Bob turned it north. He picked up a bit of speed on the narrow, winding trail even though it was rough and bumpy. Jeff hoped his dogs had heard him, but even if they had, would they be able to run the distance this man would drive? How far would this killer take them? Would the dogs be able to even catch up at all? Would they be able to keep on the trail? And if they caught up, what would prevent them from getting shot to death by this man with no conscience? Jeff was able to see the odometer from where he was sitting. Bob was doing between thirty to forty kilometres an hour at times, when the road was not too curving or too rough. In some spots, it was too uneven, and he slowed down to a crawl.

His mind went back to Eileen. She was still sitting where he had found her, unconscious. Her body was swaying and jerking with the van's movements over the uneven trail, staying upright only by the tension in the rope that bound her hands, once again, behind her back and to the wall. Her head slumped forward.

Sitting tied up on the passenger side of the van, with his back to the wall, and his hands tied to one of the brackets, Jeff had time to think. What in the world had happened? In one short morning, his life had turned upside down. Even though he'd woken up that morning with the cold feeling of emptiness and pain that he had, to some extent, gotten used to, this was a new feeling. Now he felt alone in a different sort of way. Fear gripped his heart. This madman had talked as if killing him, which Jeff believed was actually his plan, was simply a matter of convenience.

If life had been devoid of meaning and painful before, it had had a lot of meaning compared to this. And he had been looking forward to a good hunt. Now he was embroiled in a situation where he felt he would lose his life, unless a miracle happened. Again, he looked at the interior of the van. It had been stripped, just a metal shell. His thoughts, again, went to his desire for freedom. He needed to find a way to break free. Perhaps he could distract the driver or, if nothing else, get some information.

"Where are you going?" Jeff asked, above the noise of the rattling van and its motor, as Bob kept guiding the Safari northward. Jeff noticed that the driver, momentarily, looked a bit surprised and unsure of himself, as if he had not expected Jeff to be awake and asking questions. But he quickly regained his self-confidence.

"That is none of your business. Dead people don't need answers," he responded testily, and impatiently.

Jeff was persistent. "Why did you kidnap this woman, and what are you planning to do? You are breaking the law. You will face the consequences when you get arrested. Doesn't the prospect of life in prison mean anything to you? And what exactly did this woman do to you to make her your target?" Jeff was exerting effort, trying to speak above the noise and clatter of the moving van. His head was still hurting from the blow that had knocked him out.

"Look," Bob responded angrily, "don't ask so many questions. If I want to be, I can be what you'd call 'nice.' But I don't have to be. You see, I am my own man. I play by no one's rules except my own. I believe in the survival of the fittest." He seemed to mellow out a bit as he continued. "And if you die, and I survive, that just means I was the fittest." Then he let out a bellow of laughter that sounded so evil it made Jeff shudder. Jeff had, in times past, wondered what a truly evil man would be like. He was finding out in a rude way. But he could not give up. He had to keep trying.

"What are you afraid of, Bob?" Jeff asked again. "Why are you going northward, away from civilization? You got the real-estate agent, you got me, but for what?"

"You will see, you will see." Bob responded, still sounding a bit impatient, but a bit more relaxed this time. Jeff hoped that he would be able to at least reason with this man somewhat.

"Are you going to kill us?" Jeff asked, remembering too late that he had already asked that.

Bob's response was heated. "Shut up, you already asked that. Besides, that is my business and mine alone. It is none of your business." Then his facial features relaxed again, somewhat.

Jeff watched the man keenly, from where he was sitting tied up. The ride was rough and bumpy, but he was going to do his best to keep the man behind the wheel busy with more things than just his driving.

Presently, Bob spoke again, in a more civilized way. "Look, I don't leave trails. I finish my projects. It would not work for me to leave living, unfinished projects behind. Because they could get me in trouble, you see. I have never allowed a single one to live, and I won't allow you to live either. When I'm ready, I will kill you. And if I am in what you call a 'good' mood, I might decide to kill you in a pain-free way. How would you like that?" Jeff could see, from where he sat in the back of the van, that Bob almost smiled as he spoke, and continued looking ahead.

Jeff shuddered, not from cold but from reaction to what the man behind the wheel had said. Jeff still wore his jacket, with the Leatherman tool in its pocket, and thought of the knife in his winter boot. "If only I could get to my tools," he thought, "if only I was not bound, I might be able to tackle and win against this maniac."

They drove on for what seemed far too long to Jeff. After driving for some time, Eileen began to stir and moan. The left side of her face had swollen up even more, and one of her eyes was bruised as well. She raised her head and looked around in confusion. Jeff kept his gaze on her, knowing that, eventually, their eyes would meet. As soon as they did, Jeff slowly nodded his head, gently closed and opened his eyes, and then pursed his lips to form the word 'shhhh.' With a side motion of his head, he gestured toward the front of the van, toward the driver.

Eileen understood. She had immediately come to, as soon as she saw Jeff and realized where she was, and what had happened. Jeff wanted to talk to her, but was afraid of Bob. For now, Bob was driving, and it was best not to disturb him. He had hurt Eileen badly, and Jeff didn't want anything to happen to set Bob off again.

Jeff looked at Eileen and she returned his look. Jeff formed the word; "pray," and then looked upward, as if through the ceiling of the van, and into the sky.

Eileen looked puzzled. She shrugged her shoulders, and raised her eyebrows up as if to question what he meant.

Again, Jeff focused his eyes on hers and mouthed words at her. "It's okay ... it's okay." It seemed that Eileen understood because she nodded her head.

As the van continued northward, out of the front windshield Jeff could see the hills getting steeper. It was full daylight, but still cloudy. There was less wind out here in the steeper terrain. Instead of the gentle rolling hills that they had left behind, where he had stumbled upon this problem, Jeff could see now rocky terrain and, in the distance, denser forest. This logging road, no doubt, wandered a lot farther north yet, but he wished it would end already. For what seemed to Jeff like another ten minutes, the van kept climbing into the hilly country. Then, almost as if by surprise, the van veered sharply to the left, down a narrow trail toward a valley.

There was no road here, just two sets of grassy tracks. After a short distance of steep descent, they came to a clearing by a small creek. It was well sheltered. One thing Jeff was certain of was that this place would be sheltered from everything, cell phone signals, and from aircraft overhead if they should start searching. It was alarmingly obvious that the situation, for Jeff and Eileen, was even more dangerous now than it had been before. Here Jeff and Eileen would be on their own with this evil man, who had said he was going to kill them. The thought crossed Jeff's mind that death was a certainty for him and Eileen, unless a miracle would happen. But again, his mind rebelled. He just could not allow this to happen. There must be a way out, and he had to find it.

The van jerked to a halt close to some large evergreen trees. Bob turned off the ignition and leaned back in his seat. "Here we are. This will be our home for the next while." He spoke as if with a sense of satisfaction.

"Will you untie us please?" asked Jeff, "We need to stretch, we need water, and we need to just move around."

Bob turned sideways in the driver's seat, facing toward the passenger side and reached for his 12 gauge propped up by the passenger seat. He fingered his gun, and checked it, making sure it was loaded. He glanced back toward Jeff and Eileen. "Look here," he said, "I told you I am the boss, and I do as I please. If I decide to give you some freedom, I do so. If I decide not to give you any freedom, I don't."

Eileen was in visible distress. She needed to be untied and let free. "Look Bob," Jeff again spoke up, "Eileen needs some movement. She needs a break. She needs water. Can't you just have some pity?"

Bob looked at Jeff and yelled "Shut up!" He was clearly angry and looked like he was dangerously close to losing it all together. "I told you no one tells me what to do. I do as I please. I am going to have some entertainment for myself with this woman, and I will not let you spoil it for me."

Then, as if something came over Bob, his facial features softened again. "You know," he said, and he talked as if he was talking almost as much to himself as to Jeff and Eileen, "I have done this before. You are not my first killings." Turning to Jeff again, he continued, "Do you remember the disappearance of Mrs. Ivy Davis, back two years ago? I spent a week with her before I ended her life. And then, before that, the dental hygienist the paper reported missing? She was that 20 something blonde. Well, that was me too. And there have been others, and you won't be the last. This is my life."

Jeff couldn't stand it any longer. He remembered those stories, but because there was no connection to his life he had not paid close attention to them when they happened. His mind whirled, as he tried to figure out what was happening. He realized, with a fearful awareness, that his situation, and Eileen's, was worse than he had imagined. With increasing dread he became aware that he was actually in the hands of a true, professional, serial killer. This man was a man who killed for entertainment and sport! He had to do something. He spoke up. "But why, Bob? Why do you torture and kill perfectly innocent people?"

"You want to know something?" Bob responded, glancing sideways to the back from the driver's seat; "Life means something else to me than to other people. I believe in what I feel. No one can take that away from me. I just happen to have a craving for pain and death, in the lives of others, that is. In my world, the fittest survive and the weak die. The strong live off the weak. That is how it is. That is how it has always been. I just happen to be one of the strongest."

Jeff hoped he would be able to at least bring this man to some kind of reasoning. "Look Bob, I believe that everyone has value, all of us ... you, me, Miss Benson ... Her life means something. Me, I'm a man who has value, and you, Bob ... your life has value too. Don't you agree?"

Bob chuckled. "Of course. Of course I believe that life has value. Why else would I do what I do? Sure, her life has value to me, lots of value. She is my recreation. She is my entertainment. She is the source of the satisfaction of my needs, you know?" Bob's evil humour was lost on Jeff, as he saw Bob smile. It made Jeff's mind spin. This was something totally out of his comprehension. He would have never believed people like this even existed until today. And now, he found his life in the hands of one of them.

"No, I don't mean it in that way," Jeff responded, desperately. "What I mean is that her life has value in the sense that you should protect her, look out for her and treat her as a being of value, for her sake. Don't you see?"

"If I believed that, I would not be in the business I'm in, would I?" Bob replied. He spoke almost normally this time. "When I was a young boy, going to school, my life was not easy. I learned very early on that you win by fighting. The only way I ever got ahead was by taking what I wanted, and fighting for it if needed. Another thing I learned," Bob continued, "is that we who call ourselves humans are just another form of life, one that has an intellectual edge over other life forms, whatever that means. That may one day change, and other life forms may surpass humans. Who knows? But till then, I will not even think of anything else. I have made for myself a system that works for me. No one will take that away from me.

In my world, I make my own rules. The laws of society have value to society only because society has the power to enforce them. When they cannot be enforced, they mean nothing," Bob spoke matter-of-factly.

Jeff didn't like the way this discussion was going. "Don't you believe in good and evil, in right and wrong?"

Sounding a little more agitated, Bob retorted. "No, I don't. Right and wrong are human inventions that will not survive. As far as I'm concerned, what you call 'right and wrong' has never existed. It is nothing more than a part of human evolution, and it will not last. In reality, there is no right and wrong. Therefore I have no qualms about killing you. In fact, I have less feeling about killing people than you have at killing a deer. No. let me rephrase that. You kill deer for food. I kill people to feed my inner desires. To me, it's all the same. You see, I torture and kill for entertainment, for pleasure. It gives me a rush, an inner sense of satisfaction and fulfilment to see people suffer and then to see them die. I do as I please. What is the difference between you killing a deer, eating the meat, or me killing a human being for pleasure? We both get something out of it, right?"

Jeff was too stunned to even respond. This was so far off his mental radar that he didn't have a response for it. Before he could come up with something to say in return, Bob spoke again.

"There are just a few things I can't do," Bob continued. "Things like, uh, like letting you go free. If I release you, you may want to kill me or, at the very least, get back to civilization and come after me with what you call 'the law'. That is why I have to kill you if I want to survive. For your sake, when you found this woman this morning, it would have been better for you if you had ignored the scream and walked away. But such is chance."

Bob abruptly stopped talking and turned back toward the front. Next, he got out of the driver's seat, with the shotgun in his hand, and came around the van and opened the side door, making no comment and giving no explanation. Jeff figured it must be getting close to noon. But he had no way of telling for sure. He couldn't check his cell phone to check the time.

"Could we have something to drink, please?" Jeff asked, thinking again of Eileen who, being awake now, was shaking like a leaf on a tree—from pain, fear and cold. "Also," Jeff added, "could you allow me to take off my jacket and give it to Eileen? She is freezing."

"Ho, whoa, what have we here?" Bob laughed. "Are you being a gentleman now? You really puzzle me. I see you have what is called ... now, let me see ... it's called 'compassion.' Yeah, that's it, compassion. I don't know the last time I saw it. It just gets you in trouble, believe me. Compassion is for fools. Oh yes, I remember. My mother ... my mother had compassion. Oh, did she ever have compassion. She wouldn't hurt a fly. She always wanted to help 'the needy,' as she called them. She never stood up for herself, ever. But it did her in. Doing what she called 'deeds of compassion' is what killed her. She never even made it to her forty-fifth birthday. My father didn't have compassion, and still doesn't to this day. He fought for what he wanted, and he has always lived an easy life. He has outlived my mother by thirty years already. My father has never showed weakness, and it was my father who taught me how to stand up for myself and get what I wanted. I learned early on in life not to show weakness."

Jeff hated the way this man talked, and was repulsed by it. "I just want to do what is right. Could you untie our hands, and allow me to give Eileen my coat?" Jeff asked, trying to shift the focus. "She needs help. I want to give her my jacket".

Bob looked at Jeff for a moment. Jeff was not sure what Bob would do. Would he lose it? Had he pushed him too far? To his surprise, Bob complied. "I will untie your hands, but your feet will remain bound." Bob untied Jeff's hands with one hand, and kept the gun aimed at him with the other. With Jeff being 6'6" and 225 pounds, he could make quick work of Bob if given the chance. For a brief moment Jeff was tempted to take his chance and grab Bob and hold on to him, and force him to free his feet too. But it was too risky. With one trigger pull Bob could fire the shotgun at him, and he didn't want to risk it. Jeff quickly got out of his jacket and handed it to Bob. Bob took the jacket and threw it toward Eileen. With Jeff now free from the van except for his feet, Bob told him to turn sideways and put his hands behind his back again. If Jeff would make so much as a move, he would die, Bob told him. Bob tied him up again.

Jeff wished he had a way of overpowering Bob. Hopefully, his time would come before he decided to kill them. Bob untied Eileen's hands and allowed her to put on the Jacket. Then Bob tied her up again and turned to walk away. With a backward glance, he commented. "I allowed her to have your jacket for my sake, not hers. I want her to last, and not suddenly die on me. You know." It sent chills up Jeff's spine.

Jeff looked at Eileen and she tried to smile a weak 'thank you' back to him. Jeff hoped he would find a way to break free from his bonds and escape this place. But he was afraid things would get worse before they got better. Bob left Jeff and Eileen tied up in the van and walked away, down toward the creek.

Chapter 4

Jeff looked at Eileen. Together, they heard the sounds of footsteps walking away. When Jeff believed Bob was out of earshot, he spoke. "Eileen, how are you doing?"

"How do you think I'm doing?" she answered, emotionally. "Look at me. I have never been a more miserable and scared wretch. Now I already almost wish this evil monster would just go ahead and kill me and end it. That beating I got, after he knocked you out, was horrible. My shoulders ache, my whole body hurts, and my head just throbs with pain. When he was beating me, he told me that he was just starting. He said he didn't want to kill me too quick. That was just before he knocked me out. I'm sure he will kill us. There is no stopping this man. What I fear more is what he will do before he kills us."

"Let's focus on what we can do now," Jeff responded. "We have to find a way to outsmart him and get out of here. If we can get away, perhaps we can find a way to save our lives."

"If you get free, what are you going to do?" Eileen asked. "You heard him, he has killed before. He will kill us, and he will kill again."

Jeff's shoulders sagged. "You're right Eileen, we have to find a way to get out, and not only that, we have to try to apprehend him and bring him to justice. That is the right thing to do."

"How are you going to his gun away from him, *IF* you manage to break free?" Eileen asked.

"I'm working on it." Jeff responded. "What are our options? If we get free, and escape, that leaves him out here, free to go back and continue his killing spree. And we have to walk for at least a day or so to get back to my truck. We cannot take that chance. We must find a way to break free and apprehend him. I want him to face the law. Taking him in could shed light on more than a few unsolved cases. We don't know how many cases this man is involved in. Part of the reason he is talking so openly about his past is because is completely confident that both of us, you and me, are as good as dead. If only I could get out of these ropes and this chain, and get my rifle, I could gain control of him. I have no intentions of killing him, but I want to do my part get him to stop the killings. He needs to be brought to justice."

"Look Eileen," Jeff went on. "I have to try something. You and I both know that he will come back. I will complain to him that I have cramps and ask if he can let me walk around a bit. I will tell him that I am not used to sitting, much less being tied up, and that this being tied up is just killing me. I will call him a coward. Hopefully, I will be able to wound his pride by calling him a coward for keeping us tied up. Hopefully, then he will release me to prove to me, and himself, that he can control me. If I get free, I will do my very best to find a way to distract and confuse him. I realize I may end up dying, but that is our only chance."

"I don't think it will work," Eileen said desperately. "I think we're goners. You heard him. He has killed before, and who knows how many he has killed. He is a professional at this. People like you and me, just normal citizens, are like mice in a cage in a situation like this. We are powerless, completely helpless."

Jeff didn't like the way Eileen was talking, but realized that she was just being honest. "You can't give up, Eileen. You got to have faith, and pray," Jeff responded.

Eileen looked up, with a new look of surprise, a different kind of surprise. Not so much one of fear, but of disdain. "Faith? Pray?" Eileen asked incredulously. "Did I hear you right? Did you say pray? I don't believe I'm hearing this! This is crazy! How can this be happening? I don't believe in anything except what I can see. I sure hope you are not one of those religious fanatics who thinks that there is a God somewhere looking over humanity, that he is in control, and ... and ... oh yeah, that he loves us and has a 'wonderful plan' as the religious nuts say." If Eileen had spark, this was it. She was fierce.

"Look," she continued in an almost wildly desperate way, "this religious nonsense means nothing to me. I have heard enough of it to last a lifetime, but never once have I seen it work. And, of course, I'm sure your so called God has a plan in all of this as well, doesn't he? Well you just explain to me what good can come out of a mess like this? If I was God, this would not happen. I would kill vermin like this Bob on the spot."

It was clear that Jeff had hit a sensitive spot in Eileen's heart. He had not anticipated such a blowout from her. She was not finished, and went on.

"I don't buy that religious nonsense. It is nothing more than a fancy imagination, and don't try any of it on me. If there is a God of some kind somewhere, why didn't he stop this? Why doesn't he stop it now? Goodness, I can't believe this. I'm kidnapped, and now I'm stuck with some religious fool who thinks God can help it. This is unbelievable!" Jeff was hoping she would just stop already, but still she continued on. "If you believe in 'God' as you call it, tell me, what has he done for you? How has he helped you in this situation? I've been told that God loves everyone, all people everywhere. He sure doesn't love me. If he did love me and if he is watching right now he would do something. He does not love. No, he does not love at all. If he loved he would do something. Yeah, I remember now. I once heard someone say on the radio, some religious nut, that 'love is action.' If God is 'love' as you think, tell me why is he not 'doing' something?"

Jeff listened silently paying rapt attention to Eileen as she spewed forth her disgust at religion. Her mouth was like a fire hose spewing a sewer of bitter resentment toward what she understood as "God," as the words just kept pouring out. Then she suddenly stopped just as suddenly she had begun.

Jeff prepared his mind to respond, but paused. This was more difficult than he expected. "Look, Eileen," he began. "Let's not argue about religion now, okay? You and I are both facing death if Bob has his way with us. Here is what I'm thinking. I think he is more interested in you than me. Bob kidnapped you, but had no intentions of kidnapping me. In fact, he most likely doesn't even want me in the picture. You are his true target. I am in this fix because I stumbled onto the crime scene and he has to get rid of me to cover his tracks. Therefore, most likely, he will kill me before you. After he kills me, he will have his, uh, what he calls 'entertainment' with you, and finish you off too. Remember, he said that he has killed before, and that he *will* kill us.

"Eileen," Jeff continued. "After he is done with both of us, there will no doubt be a search made for us because we are missing, but after a while the search will die down, things will return to normal again, and then he will go to a different town and find another victim. Do you want that? No. We have to find a way to stop this man. Let's focus on what we have in common for now ... and what we have in common is the risk of losing our lives, and our desire to live and keep this from happening again." Jeff looked at her, waiting for a response.

Eileen seemed to gather her thoughts. "I know what you mean," she replied more calmly. "Honestly, I am afraid it's over, but I don't want to accept it yet. If you want to take a chance, or believe you have something that might work, let's go for it. Right now, it seems that the worst thing to do is nothing." She paused for a moment, and then continued. "I do hope we get free, but then, after I get back to civilian life, I don't want to see any man ever again, not one. I'm sick and tired of men." Her voice was rising again. "I have had more than enough horrid nightmarish experience with men. Over the last few days I have asked myself countless times why I ever went alone to show the house to this man in an isolated rural place and how stupid it was of me to take that chance. I could just kick myself for being so stupid."

Jeff wondered what must have happened to this young woman for her to make such reactive statements against religion, against men, and herself. It was very obvious that by suggesting prayer he had hit on a core issue in her deeper being. He realized that now was not the time, however, for those kinds of discussions. Jeff reasoned that for now he had other things on his mind, trying to focus on not getting killed, and if opportunity allowed, he would visit this subject some other time with her, in less threatening circumstances.

"Okay," Jeff responded. "Let's just concentrate on getting free now. If he unties me, and my plan works, I will do my utmost to find a way to overpower and disarm him. I don't have intentions of hurting or killing him, as much as I sense a part of me wanting to just get even with him. I just hope that I can gain control of him before he kills one or both of us."

Eileen listened and nodded. But it was clear that she had her doubts.

After what seemed like a long time the sound of footsteps could be heard again. Bob was coming back. He was coming from behind the van and, as he moved beside the open sliding door, Jeff saw that he had gathered up a large armload of firewood, and was planning on making a fire.

Jeff saw this event as an opportunity. "Bob, please, I need to stretch my legs. I need to walk around a bit. Could you untie my legs for just a short while, and also my hands? This sitting is too much for me. I'm not used to it, it's killing me."

Bob seemed to pay no attention, as he just walked past the van a short distance and threw the wood down in a clear area where there was no grass. Then he proceeded to make a fire with bits of dry twigs and leaves. In a matter of minutes, a fire was burning well. Jeff thought it was a good thing, to start a fire. If someone was looking, they might spot it. But then, who would be looking this far north?

Next, Bob walked over to the van, appearing as though he was planning to get something from the van. Jeff spoke up. "Look Bob, you are a coward. You say that you believe in the survival of the fittest. But you know something? You are a coward. It is because of people like you that we have to have law and order. If you were as fearless, as self-confident, as you claim to be, you would have no problem showing your strength by allowing me some space to move around. It's obvious that you are afraid of me, of what I could do. Why else would you keep me tied up? Strong people can live with risk, with danger. Cowards have to keep their victims in prison. Cowards like you are afraid. That is why they do things like you do." Jeff stopped, hoping Bob's pride would be wounded. Bob's next action surprised Jeff.

"Okay," Bob began. "You want to walk around a bit? Good, I will let you walk around a bit, because you have lived long enough. You said you wanted to stretch your legs. Good. Soon your legs will be permanently stretched. You are an interruption in my plans. I will let you walk for a bit, and then I will kill you." Bob said the words in such a calm, matter-of-fact manner that it again sent shivers up and down Jeff's spine. Bob kept the shotgun at the ready, as he reached down, with his left hand, under the rug behind the driver seat and pulled out a wire cutter. With a few snaps, he cut through the strands of mechanics wire that held the chain to the van floor. Jeff's feet were free. But his hands were still tied behind his back and to the inside of the van. Next Bob reached out with his left hand and undid the knot that held Jeff's hands to the van, all the while keeping the shotgun ready in his right. Jeff's hands remained tied together, but at least now he was free to move about. Jeff knew that now was not the time to try anything. He would have to wait a bit. Bob motioned Jeff to get out of the van. Jeff clumsily moved around and got out of the van, trying to balance himself, with his hands still tied behind his back.

"Face away from the van and start walking," Bob barked. Jeff complied. He walked unsteadily forward for a moment. "Stop," Bob spoke again. "I will show you that I'm in control and that I fear no one." Bob came up behind him and sliced through the ropes with a knife. Jeff was free. The sitting for so long had been hard on his legs but, after some steps, he felt the blood begin surging through his veins. It felt good to stretch his legs.

Bob spoke again; "If you want to die pain free, do as I say. If not, I will torture you." Jeff didn't believe a word this man said. He was worse than an animal and he felt Bob was saying that only to tease him and play with him, as a cat plays with a mouse.

Jeff took a few steps away from the van, uncertain as to what to do next, knowing the shotgun was trained on him. He knew he had to do something quick. Never in his life had he wanted to kill another human being, but now he realized that, if he wanted to stop the serial killing, he may not have a choice. He decided that he would do what it took to put an end to Bob's killing. He wished he was within reach of his 30-06, but he knew he would never get to it before Bob would fire on him. It was too risky. Jeff was very much aware that his options didn't look good. For the next few minutes, he would have to go along with Bob, hoping to figure out a way of turning the tables, hoping that an opportunity would present itself to him before Bob killed him. His heart pounding with adrenaline and fear, Jeff kept thinking about the fact that, if he was killed, Eileen would die too, and after her, how many more innocent lives? He had to do something. Jeff decided to engage Bob in discussion, attempting to distract him, and hopefully getting an opportunity to come up with something. Jeff stalled for a moment. Bob's response came quick.

"Move," Bob ordered angrily. "You and I are going for a walk. Walk toward the creek, and through to the other side".

"Where are you taking me?" Jeff asked.

"You have caused me a disruption in my plans. I didn't plan to come this far north this time. I sometimes come here but this time my plans were not to do so. Where you found me this morning was where I planned to do my work on this project, but you interrupted me and so, to prove to you I am for real, after you came along I decided to come back here to my old haunts. To prove to you that I mean what I say, and do what I plan, I will show you something before I kill you. You think I'm a coward. Perhaps you think that, but I will show you that

I have no more regard for a human than I do for an animal." Bob spoke with such matter-of-fact finality about killing people that it chilled Jeff each time again the words came.

Bob continued talking, as if to no one in particular; "When I was brought up, I was taught in school and by my father that I am nothing more than the product of chance, and I live as such. I was told to follow my feelings, and I learned that it feels good to follow my feelings. When I kill someone, it makes me feel in control, on top of the world. I like that. Where I will take you, you will see some things that will explain a lot of things to you, but I won't let you take that information back to the law, or 'civilization' as you would call it. That information will die with you. You are a menace to my way of life, and you have to go. Now move it."

Jeff obeyed. He walked forward, heading toward the creek. His mind raced. What was he to do? Just die? He looked at the creek. It was not far. It was only a small creek, about 20 feet wide and not very deep. It would be easy to wade through if he watched his steps. In a heavy rainfall, this creek would be a raging torrent. But now it was shallow, lazily babbling and gurgling its way over the shallow bottom, in the late fall before freezing up. In some spots there were sizable round rocks sticking up through the water. Jeff figured he might be able to use them as stepping stones. His mind continued to whirl. A thought came to him. "If Bob has me walk through the creek, there is a chance that when he steps into the water, or onto one of the rocks, he will momentarily shift his focus to keep his balance. In that split second, I have to act." As he walked closer to the creek, he asked Bob again, "Where are you taking me?"

"I'm going to make you walk up the other side of the creek, up that hill," Bob said. "There is something I want to show you. See those boulders up there to your right?"

Jeff looked up the incline in the direction Bob pointed. "Yes, I see."

"Well, among those rocks, there is a shelter where I am taking you. It is a place I have been before, and where you will go now. The walk you are taking now will be the last walk of your life." Bob said those words with such finality that it made Jeff's stomach, again, turn with fear.

They were getting close to the creek now. Jeff looked for a spot that was muddy on the other side, and perhaps slippery. He saw ahead, across the creek and a bit off to his right, that there was some mud on the opposite bank that looked like it might give him an opportunity. As he approached the bank, his mind drifted back to his childhood days as a country boy, living on the farm.

He had grown up as a person who loved nature, who loved people and who loved life. Life to him was special. His father had said to him that all of life was a gift from God, and meant to be valued and treasured. But the situation he was now facing was something he could never have imagined in his wildest nightmares. As a young boy, and later as a young adult, and now in the prime of his life, he had never thought he would one day actually plan and calculate how he might over-power and, perhaps, try to kill another human being. Feeling compelled by a power he had not known before in his life, he realized even when life hurt with the emptiness of the loss of his wife, how very much he wanted to live. Not only did he want to live, he wanted others to live too. But, in these moments, he was not sure if he wanted Bob to live anymore, or did he? He wanted Bob to live, but not at the expense of more innocents being killed. As Jeff walked toward the creek, he reigned in his thoughts again. He had to maintain focus, and control, and discipline himself. The next several minutes may well be the deciding points, not only in his life, but in the lives of more innocent victims in the future.

As Jeff got to the edge of the creek, he stepped into the water. His hunting boots were water tight up to 10 inches and in some spots the water was not even that deep. He realized to his relief that the bottom was actually quite rocky, more so than he had expected. He would do his best to just keep his hands by his sides and place his steps as if the bottom was level ground. In reality, he sensed his boots slipping a bit on some of the round and larger rocks. Jeff was pleased with that, and he hoped Bob would not notice that the bottom was uneven until he stepped in the water. Jeff made slow steady progress through the shallow water. As he went through with steady steps and started toward the other side, he listened for Bob entering the water.

In those brief moments in the creek, Jeff knew he had to act. He made the decision that he would risk everything and use whatever force it would take to subdue this madman if he could. Jeff knew the shot gun was trained on him, and without a doubt, his life was about to be ended if Bob had his way. He had to do something, and if he did, it would be in the next few moments.

Jeff listened for Bob stepping into the water. He hoped that, when he did, for a split second he would look at where he was placing his foot, and maybe have to pay attention, for a moment, to his balance. That would be his chance.

Jeff was, by now, close enough to the other side to reach down and touch the soft mud of the bank. He slowed his movement. He heard Bob's first step in the water among the rocks. On the second step, he would take his chance. Jeff didn't dare look back at Bob, in case he was paying close attention to him.

At the exact moment when Jeff heard Bob's second foot enter the water he went into action. He bent over, at lightning speed, turning toward his left and, with one swooping motion, grabbed a handful of mud with his right hand, while dropping to his knees. As he was turning and going down, he flung a large fistful of mud straight into Bob's face. His guess had been right. Bob had found the bottom uneven and had momentarily shifted his focus to where he was stepping, holding his arms stretched out, balancing himself as though he were walking a beam. Bob's right hand was holding the shotgun out to the side as he was steadying his steps in the water.

Bob was about fifteen feet behind him, but the soft cold mud had found its mark and landed square in his face, just as he raised his eyes his eyes from focusing on where he was stepping. Bob reeled backward, and went sideways from the imbalance, blinded by the mud in his face. He fell heavily. Jeff was down too now, on his knees in the mud, but in an instant Jeff grabbed another scoop of mud in his big bulky hand, and, rising to his feet, aimed straight for Bob's face again, where it hit with full force.

Bob had regained his senses in an instant and realized what was happening. His victim was trying to get away. In confusion, as he was going down, Bob had pulled the trigger and the shotgun blasted its charge harmlessly upward, at an angle toward the sky, almost flying out of Bob's hand from the recoil. But he held onto the gun. In the next instant, Bob also realized he had missed his target. He tried to get the mud out of his eyes, and reload the shotgun at the same time, struggling to pull the choke to reload another round into the chamber. But he was too late.

Jeff came down heavily on top of Bob, all two hundred and twenty five pounds of him. With his right hand, he grabbed Bob's throat and pushed him down on his back, burying Bob's head under the water and pressing it into the rocky creek bottom. If Jeff wanted, he could drown this maniac right then and there, get rid of the body, and no one would ever need to know. Jeff was strongly tempted, to hold Bob's head under and let the water do its work. Bob struggled hard and resisted fiercely, but was no match for the big, broad-shouldered, metal worker who had for years built up his strength handling the heavy sheets. With one hand Jeff held him down like a vice, keeping his head under water and choking off his air at the same time. With his left hand, Jeff grabbed the shotgun and wrested it out of Bob's hand.

One shot had been fired, but Bob had not had time to pull the choke to reload. Jeff knew that that particular gun could hold five shells, and now it was in his hands. Jeff continued holding Bob underwater for a few more moments. He was strongly tempted to loosen his grip on Bob's throat enough so that he could inhale some water. His thoughts wrestled with his feelings. Part of him wanted to let the water fill Bob's lungs and make an end of him. But he could not force himself that far. Killing Bob was not his goal, but a last resort. Jeff lifted him a bit, until his head appeared above water, and loosened his grip enough to let Bob breathe. Spitting water, Bob gasped for air.

"Look Bob," Jeff said, panting from adrenaline and anger, "I guess it's the survival of the fittest now, is it? According to your way of life, I should kill you, and I can do it now if I want to. How about that?" Jeff was lungs were heaving from anger, and the realization of how close he had been to getting killed by this madman ... and how easily he could now end this madman's life.

"Look, Bob ... listen here. If I followed my feelings right now, as you follow yours, I would end your life with my bare hands. All I need to do is keep you under water for a few minutes and you would be dead. Or, I can take one of these rocks here and bash your skull in. I have the chance and I have the power. But I'm not like you. I will try not to kill you. But tell me, Bob, why should I let you live?" Inwardly, Jeff continued to fight hard with the temptation to kill the man on the spot. His mind raced again. He had plenty of options. He could just hold Bob's head under water and let nature take its course. He could bash his skull in, or he could shoot him if he wanted to. Or, with one solid blow of his large fist he could knock him out, turn him on his face, and leave him there, drowning while he was out.

"Answer me," Jeff fairly shouted at Bob. "Why should I let you live, after what you did to Eileen, and now to me, and what you said you did to your other victims?"

Bob was not responding. He continued gagging and spitting water and mud from his mouth. Jeff gripped the shotgun tightly in his left hand, released his grip on Bob's throat with the other, and jumped off of him. Moving away, he stepped a short ways out of the creek. He had decided to avoid killing Bob if he could. But he was going to bring Bob in to face justice.

"Now you do as I say, or I will kill you." Jeff said evenly, as he levelled the shotgun at Bob, pulled the choke and reloaded a round. "Get on your feet and start walking. You lead me to the place where you wanted me to go. One suspicious move and I will kill you. That information you wanted me to know, before you were going to kill me? That information is what I want to know. Now, we are going to have a look-see, so I can take you along with me when I take Eileen back to town. You will face the law."

Jeff decided he better put some space between himself and Bob, in case Bob had a plan, but he wanted to be within firing range in case Bob tried something. Jeff was going to make Bob walk up to the place where he said he wanted him to go, and check it out. Jeff suspected that there might be something there. Then, when he had seen what he wanted, he would bring Bob back down, figure out a way to tie him up, and get him to the police.

"Get moving," Jeff barked. He was not used to treating another human being this way. In his world, he had always believed in treating people with respect and courtesy. But he realized that to stop this madman from killing more people, and for his own safety, there was no other way than to use the man's own language to communicate—and the language of choice for this criminal was physical force and power.

Bob got up and waded through the creek, walking in the direction Jeff had instructed. He went slowly up the incline, as if stalling for time. Sopping wet and muddy, he was beside himself with rage. A cornered tiger looked friendly compared to the face Bob displayed. Jeff knew that if Bob gained control at this point, his life would be over in an instant, and Eileen would fare worse since he would take everything out on her. Jeff had never seen a human being more animal-like than this man. It was like he was possessed. Jeff held the shotgun trained on Bob, at eye level. Jeff didn't know how many rounds of ammo were in the gun. If the magazine had been full, then he had five more. Jeff still had no intention of killing Bob, but decided he would, if it came to it. Whether or not Bob would die would depend on his cooperation with Jeff. This had gone far enough.

Slowly, the two made their way up the slope with Bob leading the way about fifteen feet ahead. Jeff knew that he could not afford to take his eyes off Bob for even an instant. He had to make sure he would see what Bob had wanted him to see, and he had to make sure that he got Bob back to civilization. He would have to tie him up and deliver him to the police. Even though Jeff had things under control, his heart was bounding and his breathing was heavy and sharp. Jeff knew he was out of his zone. Never in his life had he faced what he was facing now, and never had he imagined he would one day be pointing a loaded gun at another human being, threatening to shoot him if he didn't follow an order. But if Jeff was out of his zone, so was Bob. It was obvious, that for years, Bob had lived as he pleased, and he was not used to facing what he had been giving to other people. Bob had always been the one instilling fear and dread on other people. Now he faced it himself, and he was responding with rage. Jeff knew that it would take only one slip up on his part for things to turn around. He had to make sure Bob would not catch him off guard in any way, or be able to trick him. Knowing that Bob was a man with no feelings of humaneness for anyone, just rage and contempt, and had no ability to even think in a civil way, he could not be too careful. Even now, just the way Bob was reacting to Jeff was more proof of his evil nature. It was ever more clear to him that Bob was a killer, and even when facing death would not back down. Bob was a man who had lost his humanity. Jeff's mind continued racing as he kept his unblinking eyes steady on Bob. Jeff believed that if Bob was up to something, it would happen soon. They continued walking, with Bob slowly lead the way, when suddenly Bob spoke.

"So, now that you have the gun, are you going to kill me?" Bob asked, sarcastically.

"That depends on the decisions that you will make," said Jeff. "I could have drowned you in that creek back there if I had wanted to. I could have killed you then. I know that physically I am much stronger than you. Now just shut up and do as I say. Just keep on walking and show me the place where you were going to stretch out my legs permanently. I want to see that place before I take you in. If I find what I think is there, we may have some answers to some unsolved crimes."

Bob hesitated, as if stalling for time. "What if I don't show you where it is?" he asked.

"You will! Now *MOVE*!" Jeff ordered angrily. Bob began walking again. Again, Jeff realized how unaccustomed he was to this. Using force on another human being in this manner was completely foreign to him. At the same time, he realized that he had to show this man that he would kill him if he had to. He would not let him do any more harm than he already had. Bob kept walking.

"How much farther is it?" Jeff asked, keeping the shotgun trained on Bob, who was looking forward, in the direction he was walking. Jeff saw Bob's shoulders tense. Something was up. Jeff gripped the gun tightly, the barrel trained right between Bob's shoulder blades.

"See those boulders over there?" Bob asked, pointing with his left hand toward some large outcropping of rocks a short distance away. Jeff didn't respond or shift his eyes. He knew in an instant that Bob was planning a diversion tactic. He was trying to distract him and then would make a move. Of just what kind of move, Jeff was unsure. He kept the barrel of the gun aimed right between Bob's shoulders and, without moving his aim, or his eyes, asked for clarification. "Which boulders?"

What happened next was so fast Jeff couldn't even follow it. When he asked the question, Bob, his left hand still pointing toward the boulders, reached behind himself with his right hand and pulled a handgun out of his belt, from beneath his dripping winter jacket. In one continuous motion, he whirled around, and fired the gun at Jeff. Luckily, the gun was wet and, in Bob's still muddy and slippery hands, his aim was off.

Bob had underestimated Jeff. He had figured that if he pointed with his left hand toward the boulders, Jeff would shift his focus for a moment, and that that would be his chance. He had figured Jeff would make a similar mistake to the one he had made when he lost his balance in the creek. But it was not to be. When Jeff had asked the question, he had not shifted his focus. His eyes had not left Bob. He'd kept them, and the shotgun, trained right between Bob's shoulder blades. Jeff was ready. The moment Jeff saw the pistol come up and Bob whirl around to fire it, he pulled the trigger on the 12 gauge. The two guns fired so simultaneously that it was almost like one shot. Bob's turning movement had been so quick that, by the time Jeff pulled the trigger on the shot gun, Bob took the hit from the front. The shotgun fired a solid slug into Bob's chest. Bob fell forward and down like a heavy, wet sack.

Chapter 5

When the shotgun fired, Jeff had no uncertainty about whether or not he would hit his target and, knowing that, he was just not sure whether it would kill him. If he was alive, he would likely try to fire again. Instinctively Jeff reloaded, ready to fire if Bob would raise the handgun. Bob didn't stir. Jeff cautiously walked over to Bob with the shotgun at the ready. Bob still had the pistol in his hand. Jeff kicked it away from him. Bob lay on his face, very still. Blood started oozing from beneath him. Jeff waited a few moments, undecided what to do next. He bent over and felt for a pulse on his neck. There was nothing. Bob was dead.

Jeff again stood there for a moment, trembling from fear and adrenaline. As the realization of what he had just done started to slowly sink into his brain, he began shaking. He had done something he had never dreamed he would do, he had shot and killed another human being. In his whirling thoughts, he realized that now however was not the time to panic. He had gotten free, but now he had other things to tend to.

He quickly picked up the handgun and stuck it into his hip pocket. Then he grabbed the body, turned it over and closed up Bob's jacket, so as not to get himself all bloody from the wound. Then he slung the limp dead body over his shoulders and picked up the shotgun, starting back toward the van at a brisk walk. The dead man's weight felt remarkably light as he carried him toward the van. In a matter of only minutes, he was back across the creek and at the van.

He was thinking as he walked. First, he would untie Eileen, get her to stretch and move around briefly, get her some water, and then take the van and the body and head back. On the road, they could eat some of the food Bob had ransacked out of Jeff's bag and tossed into a corner in the van. Hopefully, he would make it back to town by nightfall. He dropped the dead body by the van, and jumped into the van. Eileen's face was white as chalk.

She had heard the shots and, in an instant, Jeff realized that she had thought Jeff was dead and it would be Bob coming for her. She had figured Bob had shot him and that her turn would be next. A flood of relief washed over her face as she saw that it was Jeff coming for her.

"Here, quick, let me untie you," Jeff panted from excitement and adrenaline. "Let's get out of here, and back to town."

Eileen was too stunned to respond. It was as if she was in a daze. Jeff worked, grabbing his knife out of his boot and slicing through the ropes holding her. Next, he took the multipurpose pliers from the coat he had lent her. Quickly, he cut the wires that held the chain together around her ankles and slid the chain off.

"There," Jeff said, "get out and stretch for a moment or two and then let's get out of here. Hopefully, we can make it back to town before dark."

Eileen slowly got up, and grew faint. Jeff caught her and steadied her. She let out a groan of pain. Jeff realized that she was in immense pain, and held her to steady her. Jeff helped her out of the van and sat her down on the ground.

"I'm okay, really I am," Eileen said. "Just let me walk around for a bit, and get some circulation into my limbs." Jeff helped her to her feet. He, too, was in a daze. Everything had happened as if in slow motion. The whole thing, from when they had gotten to this place until now, had not taken that long. But for Eileen, it was already several days, and it had taken its toll on her. She sat on the ground for a while and then, slowly, got up and walked around a bit. It was obvious to Jeff that she had suffered tremendously in Bob's captivity. Jeff was not sure how long he should just relax, and allow her to get some circulation through her body, before they started heading back.

It was getting into the afternoon, and daylight would start waning in the overcast November sky. The temperature was still chilly, but there was no wind in this sheltered area. Jeff just hoped that he would be able to get Eileen back to town safely.

This deer-hunting trip had turned out to be a disaster. He had killed a man, and he realized that he would have to face the law for that. His mind went to his faith community, and to his church. Unlike traditional Baptist teachings, Jeff's background was from the conservative Anabaptists who believed all forms of force and resistance was wrong. He had been brought up as a pacifist, believing that it was sin to use force on other people. They didn't believe in being part of the legal or political system, or worse, the justice system. It suddenly struck him that he would have to answer to the church leadership for this as well. He began shaking again, and wondered if this was all just a bad dream. He was not sure what bothered him more, facing the church leaders, or the reality that he had killed a man, created in the image of God. His mind whirled again. "What have I done?' He just stood there by the van for a while, trying to collect his thoughts.

After Eileen had walked around for a few moments, she came up beside him as he stood by the van. "What are you doing?" she asked.

Jeff shook his head, coming back to reality. "Nothing ... uh, just thinking," he responded. "Here, let's get that fire out and then get his body into the back of the van, and get back to town. I'll check his pockets for the keys." Jeff grabbed the jug that Bob had thrown back into the van, ran to the creek and got some water. Then he doused the fire, which had begun to die down from not being fed more wood. Next, he searched Bob's pockets and found some personal belongings. There was a set of keys, and a wallet. The wallet held some papers, but not any ID. There were also a few fifty, and hundred dollar, bills. Jeff noticed that there was no credit, or debit, card. He put the wallet back into Bob's pocket and put the keys in his. Next, he picked up the body, put it on the floor of the van, and lay the old rug blanket over it. Jeff quickly grabbed the keys from his pocket, got in the driver's seat and started the van.

"Eileen, you ready?" he asked. Eileen was busy sorting through Jeff's stuff, which lay scattered on the van floor. She took a few bottles of water and some beef Jerky, and slowly with pain got into the passenger seat. Jeff turned the van around and headed back up the hill and onto the narrow road down which they had come. He was not familiar with this territory, and would have to be careful.

His first goal was to head back to where he had found the van, first thing this morning. He would pull up onto the clearing and call for his dogs. Hopefully, they were still there. If they had decided to follow, he would meet them on the road.

As Jeff and Eileen headed south, Jeff's mind relaxed a bit. His mind kept replaying what had just happened. What a tragic day it was. Jeff could not wrap his mind around the fact that he had just killed a man, and he again shuddered at the thought of what he had done. But, at the same time, in his heart he knew that he had done the best he could with what he had to work with, and all he could do now was hope for the best.

Jeff's mind, again, went back home, to his church. How would he explain this to his church? He tried to tell himself to worry about that later but, try as he might, he was not at peace. What would the church do? He had been a recluse for so long, he had let his relationship with many of the people drift away. He was not sure what the response would be to what he had done. As far back as he knew, not one of his fellow church members had ever been part of law enforcement, politics, or the military. As conservatives and pacifists, they considered themselves called by God to be a witness for God, through their faith in Jesus, by living a lifestyle in line with Jesus' teachings—doing things like turning the other cheek when facing difficulties, giving up their rights, going the second mile, and not resisting evil people. Today he had resisted evil with force and had won. But how would the church look at it? Well, the only way to find out was to keep going on and face the circumstances head on. Jeff's mind was in turmoil as he continued guiding the van down the trail that Bob had taken them that morning.

For about a half an hour, Jeff drove with Eileen in the passenger seat. They were both silent. Eventually, Eileen spoke up. "Thank you for saving me."

"Uh, what, what did you say?" Jeff's train of thought was interrupted, and he had to shift his focus to pay attention to Eileen in the passenger seat.

"I said, thank you for saving me today," she repeated.

"Oh, yeah ... it's okay, you're welcome. I did what I felt I had to do. If I had not stumbled on your camp site this morning, on my hunting trip, I would not be here now, and you might not be either," Jeff responded.

"I'm just glad you came along when you did. When Bob abducted me, he let me know, very clearly, that I was his and that he would take me for himself."

Jeff was not sure if it was safe to ask about her experience. He needed to get Eileen to safety, and to some medical attention. There was no telling what she had experienced in the presence of her abductor. Jeff was not sure if he should ask Eileen what had happened, or just wait and let her come out with the story on her own. No doubt the authorities would question her. He decided to give Eileen a chance to talk to him about it.

"I don't mean to pry Eileen, but if you would like to talk about it, I mean about what happened, I would be interested in listening. I'm sure it must have been terrifying, On the other hand, if you are not ready to talk about it at this time, that's fine too. You can always do that later. Sometimes it helps to just get things off one's heart and into the open. I'm ready to listen if you want to talk. As I said, sometimes talking helps ease the pain inside." Jeff stopped talking, feeling that, perhaps, he had said too much already. With women he was never sure how much or how little to say. There was silence between the two for a while, as they drove on.

After a while of driving, Eileen suddenly spoke up, catching him off guard. "Several days ago, on ... I can't even remember what day of the week it was," she shook her head, "anyway, I got this phone call from a guy who called himself Bob Timmins. He said he had seen a 'for sale' sign out on a property by Pond Mill road, and that he had seen my phone number on it and decided to call me. He said he was interested in the property and asked if I could show it to him. I thought nothing of it and agreed to meet him and show it to him. When I got there, I noticed a van in the driveway and I realized that he was already there. I walked up to the house, he got out, and I greeted him, and said 'hello.' I walked up to the door and unlocked it, invited him to come in and walked in first. He followed. After we got inside …" Her voice failed her at this point.

It was clear that Eileen was struggling with her emotions as she spoke. Jeff decided to just listen attentively and keep listening. It seemed to him that Eileen needed to speak, and he wanted her to. After a few moments, Eileen continued. "After we got inside, I asked him what he was looking for in a house, what he was interested in. The next thing I realized was that he was not looking at the house at all. He was staring at me with a strange kind of glare. I instantly realized that something was wrong. I decided to pretend I was calm and composed, and simply said that I wanted to show him the living room first. I proceeded to tell him the details of the house. In my mind, I was looking for a way to get outside and make a run for my car. He freaked me out by the way he looked at me. I just knew by his look that he was dangerous. I don't know why I didn't pick that up before I went into the house, but for some reason I just wasn't aware of anything. As I went into the living room, making my way toward the door, and pretending I was showing him more of the house ... it was at that moment that I saw him move toward me in a way I have never seen a man move toward another person. He kind of lunged at me. I was scared, and rushed for the door. I wanted to get out, and to my car, and get out of there. I never made it. He grabbed my arm and held me fast. I tried getting free but I was no match for him. I struggled as hard as I could, but I was paralysed with fear."

By now Eileen was in tears, sobbing openly. The pent up emotions and fear were flowing freely now. Jeff spoke up. "It's all right, Eileen. Just let the tears flow, you have nothing to fear now. Bob is gone and will never hurt you again," Jeff said, in a soft comforting voice.

Eileen continued between sobs. "I tried so hard to get free from him. I tried to bite him. I tried to hit him but he hit me so hard on my nose that it bled instantly. The next thing I knew my whole face was bloody." Her slender body heaved with sobs.

Jeff spoke. "Well, Eileen, if you would rather not talk now, its okay. Why don't you rest for a moment? Just lean back a bit and rest. I would guess that we have a good while of driving before we'll get back to where we left this morning."

Eileen leaned back in her seat a bit, but the road was too rough to get a good position. Nevertheless, she tried. Her head leaned back, and she closed her eyes, trying to get some much needed rest.

Jeff kept on guiding the van along the narrow road, but his mind was not there with him. It kept going back to the early morning, when he had first heard the scream, and then had found her tied up in the van. He could still see her, vividly, in his mind. She had been fear stricken, hair all over her face and shoulders, and stains of blood on her sweater and pants. Jeff glanced over to Eileen, as she was leaning back with her eyes closed. The blood stains were still on her clothes, and her face was bruised. "The story is starting to take shape," Jeff thought. By a simple accident, he had stumbled onto a serial killer who was in the dirty business of abducting unsuspecting women.

The killer would abduct women he had no connection to, and, to satisfy his devilish urges, he would torture, and most likely rape them and then kill them. To his knowledge, Jeff had never heard of a serial killer who had gotten caught, who had not raped his victims. The fact that Bob was a murderer was clear to him, no doubt about that. Jeff just wondered how this case would unravel in court, if it would get to that. He hoped it would not go there. He wondered if Bob would have any relatives or close friends who would now come after him. Jeff didn't think it would take much effort convincing a jury of his innocence, and Bob's guilt, if he was prosecuted in court. Eileen could, and would, testify on his behalf if, and when, the time came. Jeff was also convinced that there were more victim's than just Eileen. He believed Bob spoke the truth when he'd told them that he had killed others. Jeff figured all he would have to do would be to guide the police back to the hill where he had killed Bob and find some more evidence. He was convinced that there would be the remains of other victims to be found there.

As the van made its way south, Jeff's mind continued to wander. The unthinkable had taken place. He had never believed that he would be involved in a murder case, least of all with him being the killer. But there was something strange about this. Even if he had killed, was he a killer? He thought about it like a person trying to find pieces to a puzzle, in which some pieces appear so strange that one wonders if they will ever fit. Could he be called a killer? No. It was Bob who was the killer. He had just stopped a killer from continuing to kill.

Jeff's mind went back to his boyhood days in Sunday school, to the time when the teacher had made him and his friends memorize the Ten Commandments. One of them was: Do Not Kill. He learned that he should not kill. He had to admit that he had killed a man. But what would have been the alternative? He knew that, when he heard the scream, right at the start, and saw the van as he came over that hill, he could have turned back, walked back to his truck and went elsewhere, and never mentioned a word. No one would have ever known. It would have been his secret to take with him to the grave. But deep down in his heart he knew that he would not have been able to live with himself, knowing that there was a possible connection between the blue van and the missing woman. And, in this case, that was exactly what had happened.

Jeff felt that he had been put in a spot where there was no pain free way out. No matter what he would have done, any response at all would have caused pain, one way or another. Simply by the nature of his character, he had been in a spot where to do nothing would have been wrong. And, in doing something, he had entered into an area of his life where he had deeply mixed feelings. By rescuing Eileen, he had wanted to do the honourable thing and help her get free from distress and certain death. His goal to rescue Eileen had been accomplished. But it had happened at the cost of the life of her abductor. Jeff wondered if, perhaps, the question was not whether he had done the right thing or the wrong thing. Perhaps the question was, did he do the best he could do under the circumstances? Jeff felt he had. "In reality," he thought, "if things are handled right by my community, I should be commended for having had the courage to risk my life in taking down this killer." His thoughts were interrupted by Eileen in the passenger seat. Obviously she was not asleep.

Eileen continued speaking where she had left off, as if no time had elapsed between when she had last spoken and the present, when in fact it had been a considerable amount of time. "When he grabbed me and dragged me backward across the floor, I tried desperately to get free. He dragged me past the big window facing the street, and I grabbed a curtain and wiped my face with it to try to make it obvious that a struggle had happened, if the police should come that way. As he dragged me toward the door, everything went black. The next thing I remember was waking up inside this van, tied up and bound, and the van was moving. I was hurting from the blow to my head, and my face was still bloody. He paid no attention to me, and just continued driving for I don't know how long. It got dark, and I was just paralysed with fright.

"That place where you found me this morning was where we spent a few nights. He would make a large fire at night and warm himself up by it. He had his rug with him and would spread it out. From time to time, he would come and look at me. I would beg him to give me some freedom to move about, and to relieve myself, and he allowed that. But he never allowed me to walk more than fifteen feet away from him. He watched my every move and kept that shotgun trained on me at all times when I was not tied up. It was so embarrassing and humiliating. Every time he came to tie me up again he had me face away from him and knocked me out with a blunt object. When I would come to again, he would talk to me. He said he wanted to save me for the right time. It seemed that he enjoyed watching my nerves wreak havoc with me. He took delight in making me wait in silence when he would walk away for extended periods of time. He knew what a torture-weapon time can be, and he used it on me powerfully. I have to say that I have never been so scared in my life. I was absolutely sure that I would die, and I am still sure that I would have died. I was convinced that there was no way I was going to make it out alive. The stories he told me of his life, what he did to those other women were so grisly, and so disturbing. Oh, the pain." She sobbed again. At this point in her story, Eileen visibly shuddered.

"I can't begin to tell you what he told me," Eileen continued again, sobbing. "I feel so sorry for those poor women he described. When he talked about them ... what he had done with them ... it was like ... like the way a friend would describe how to prepare a gourmet meal. My heart is trying to tell me that he may not have done the things he said he did."

Jeff listened, his hands on the wheel, and his mind wondering what kind of mind, inside a human body, could sink to such lows. He was glad that Eileen was talking. He could tell that she needed to get this out of her system.

Eileen went on. "I begged him to let me go. I agreed to do anything he wanted, if only he would let me live. He just laughed, and it was obvious that he was having a good time. It became obvious to me that my fear fed his cravings. The more fear I had, the better he enjoyed it. It was so scary. I have never before in my life really thought about it much, but now I am convinced, beyond any doubt, that some people are simply evil. I don't believe in spiritual things, but if there is such a thing as a devil, this man was it."

Presently Eileen turned to Jeff again. "Do you know what it feels like when your fear, your pain and your anguish, is the source of someone else's amusement?" She asked, sobbing, with tears running down her cheeks.

Jeff shook his head, trying to communicate with body language that he was understanding what she was saying "No, Eileen I don't. I have never experienced anything like what you are describing to me. I would have never guessed that such things as you describe exist. But I believe you." He finished quickly. Jeff was glad she was talking. Talking about it would help her get her emotions out into the open, and help her to heal sooner from this terrifying ordeal. "No," he said again, "I don't know what that feels like."

Eileen had spent a lot of emotion, talking about her experience, and she quieted down. It seemed to Jeff that it was best to let the subject rest. He continued driving. After a few minutes, he thought it might be good to get her thoughts onto things more related to their next course of action. Jeff decided to change the subject for now.

"What are your plans when we get to town?" Jeff asked. He was not sure himself what he was going to do. Getting the police involved would be the first step. Hopefully, he would not have to go to jail for killing a man. But, for now, he wanted Eileen to, at least, have the awareness of needing to focus on the next steps. Giving her mind something to do might be a good thing.

"I don't know what I will do," Eileen responded. "I have no idea."

"You have relatives in town?" Jeff asked.

"Not in Forest Hill," Eileen responded.

"Do you have any connections elsewhere?"

"Just the company I work for, Red Stone Realty. We are five employees altogether," she answered. "My mother lives two hours away in Poplar Ridge, south of Forest Hill. She is old and confined to a senior's home, and doesn't go out. Her mental capacities are not always there anymore."

"Do you have any brothers and sisters?" Jeff asked further, not feeling very comfortable with this much prying into this woman's life, but somehow feeling responsible for her, given her state of stress and pain. He was not sure where this woman was at in her life and he wanted to know a little bit more, if possible, in the hopes of finding a way to get her some help.

"No," Eileen responded. "I was an only child. I grew up in a single parent home."

"What about your dad?" Jeff went on. "Is he around?" Jeff realized a bit too late that he should not have asked that question. He sensed Eileen immediately tense up. She remained silent and didn't seem to want to answer. Jeff felt the awkwardness of the moment and decided to let it go.

Awkwardly, Jeff spoke again; "I'm sorry, Eileen. I really didn't mean to pry or anything. I was just concerned about getting you connected with loved ones, and getting you some help. For now, I would like to see you find a place to rest for a while. Let's get back to Forest Hill. We'll notify the police and then get you a place to sleep. Are you okay with that?"

Eileen just nodded. Something up ahead caught Eileen's attention. "Look, what are those?" She pointed straight ahead into the distance. Jeff looked up from the road in front of them, and peered farther ahead.

"Dogs!" Jeff said, excitedly. "Am I ever glad to see them. Those are my dogs!"

"You have dogs?" Eileen asked. "You never mentioned anything about dogs. I hate dogs."

"Sorry Eileen, those are my dogs," Jeff said. "They are coming with us. I left them hidden behind a big boulder this morning, when I went down to check out the van ... and Bob kidnapped me along with you. I was hoping they would follow, or stay after I got tied up too. Good thing they are coming for us. All I need now is to find the place where Bob turned onto the road this morning, when he took us north and then we should be okay."

The dogs were trotting slowly toward the oncoming van. They seemed a bit confused. Jeff slowed the van down, and pulled to a stop about a hundred feet before he reached them. He got out of the van and called his dogs. "Brick, Max, come here."

One call was all the dogs needed. They recognized their master instantly and came toward him full speed. They had missed him, and were glad to see him, that was clear. "Well, at least you are safe," Jeff said, squatting down and petting his beloved pets. "Let's get you guys in the van and go home." Jeff realized that the dogs were not aware of Eileen in the van, or of the dead body. He would have to introduce Eileen to them, and tell them to leave the body under the rug alone. "Okay boys," Jeff said. "In the van is a friend of mine. Her name is Eileen. She is a good person and I want you to be good to her. Don't scare her, you hear?" The dogs licked Jeff's face in response.

Jeff got up, walked around the van to the sliding door, and opened it. The moment he opened the door, the dogs sensed something was different. "it's okay boys, just hop in and lay down, okay?" Jeff coaxed. The dogs obeyed, jumping in and laying down behind the driver and passenger seats.

Eileen didn't say a word. She didn't like dogs, and had no intention of starting now. She didn't like animals, period.

Jeff walked around the front of the van, got back in the driver's side, behind the wheel, put the van in gear and started driving again. He was glad things were beginning to look good. After driving for a while again, his mind was wondering how far it might still be to where he had been this morning when this trouble began? As he drove on, he realized it was getting to be a bit late in the afternoon and, with the thick cloud cover and the trees around, darkness would come early. For now, he would continue driving and hope he would not miss the place where the two trees and the large rock were—Twin Pines Rock. The heater in the van was doing a good job of keeping the vehicle warm. Outside, the wind had died down and there was almost no air movement. Jeff wondered if it would begin to snow.

"This deer hunting trip has turned out to be a total disaster," Jeff thought. "I came out to Beaver's Creek to bag a deer. What I have, perhaps, bagged is going to be the biggest problem of my life. I almost got myself killed. Instead of killing a deer, I have killed a man, and now I'm driving his vehicle."

In all his years, first as a boy, and now as a man, he had never remotely thought he would be involved in a murder case, and be the killer at that. He shook his head, as if the shaking would sort out his jumbled thoughts and help them fall into place.

Jeff tried to concentrate on his driving, trying to make sure he would not bounce the van too much, for both Eileen's sake, and also because he didn't want it to break down all of a sudden on this lonely road. He continued, carefully guiding the van along the narrow, winding road. It seemed to him that he must be near where they had turned onto the road, but he could not tell for sure.

Slowly, he became aware that the rear end of the van began to ride differently, with a kind of sideways motion at times. "Maybe I'm just imagining things, or perhaps it's the terrain," he thought. But it got worse, and then it got very bumpy. He realized that it felt like he might have a flat on the van, and he slowed it down and then came to a stop. As he slowed the van down, Eileen turned and looked at him.

"I think we may have a flat tire," Jeff responded to her questioning look. He sat for a moment, with the van stopped, the engine idling, and his foot on the brake, contemplating what course of action he would take now. Putting the van in park, he got out and walked around the van. The passenger-side rear tire was flat and, from the appearance of the tire, it was obvious that he had been driving with a low tire for quite some time. "I hope the spare is full," Jeff thought. "If there is a spare."

Eileen was now out of the van too, and beside him by the rear tire. She had taken off the heavy winter coat Jeff had loaned her earlier in the day, and was now again just in her light winter coat. She stood there, arms folded tightly against her chest for body warmth, and looked at the flat tire, and then at Jeff. "Can you fix this?"

"That depends," Jeff answered. "If there is a spare in the back, and if it's full, and if there are tools to jack up the van and take off the tire, then we should be able to get going again." Jeff opened the back doors to see if he could locate the spare tire some where. The dogs were curious as to what was going on, and he told them to stay put and be quiet. They listened without protest.

This type of van was not very familiar to Jeff, and he didn't know that the spare was not in the interior of the van. After looking for a minute or so, he decided that the interior was not the place to look. "Most likely it's under the rear-end on this type of vehicle," he thought, remembering that perhaps this van was not like a car, but like a pickup truck, where the spare was usually in back, beneath the vehicle. He got down on his knees and peered under the van. It was a bit dark under there, but he could see enough. There was, indeed, a place for the spare tire underneath the rear of the vehicle. A bracket, dangling by a loose bolt, showed where the spare tire was supposed to be, but there was nothing.

Chapter 6

Jeff didn't like that the spare was missing. The fact that there was no spare tire meant one of two things. He could try to continue driving, or go the rest of the way to his truck on foot. He would have to decide.

"Is there a spare tire?" Eileen asked.

"No, just a bracket that held a spare tire at one time. But there is nothing now," Jeff answered. "Well, it looks like we are going to be stuck here for a while," he added. "I hate this situation," he muttered.

"What are we going to do now? Can't we just drive with a flat tire?" Eileen asked.

"We could drive for a little while, but not for long. Driving like this, the rubber would come off the rim and we might wreck the vehicle, or worse, have an accident—although on this road, at the slow speed we travel, that would not be a huge risk. Still, it would not be long before everything would come to a standstill. I don't know how far it still is to where we were this morning. From there, we can just walk over the ridge toward my truck. My sense is that we are not too far away from where we were this morning. As far as this van is concerned, we can't really drive it. We need to find a different way." Jeff spoke as much to himself as to answer Eileen's question. With the sky still clouded over, and with darkness near, he didn't want to chance travelling too far, passing the place where they had been in the morning, and thereby passing his truck and missing it on the other side.

Eileen looked puzzled. "You have a truck here, close by? Oh yes, I remember now. You mentioned that this morning when you found me." Then she continued. "I guess I'm at your mercy. What are you suggesting?" She asked, hesitantly.

"Well, somewhere over on the east side of this hill, is a road and, just off of that road, I have my truck," Jeff responded. "If we can just get to it, I have everything there that we need to get back to town. But now we have to concentrate on getting moving again," Jeff continued. "Here, let's do some thinking. We have some supplies. They will last us at least a full day, if need be. We have the dogs and also some winter wear to keep us warm. We can make a fire." Jeff was thinking audibly to himself, and weighing his options. He made his decision.

"Look here," he began again. "It's going to be getting dark soon, and I'm not quite sure where we are. The dogs might know the way back to the truck, but I would rather not make that trip in the dark. Also, if we travel by daylight, we have a better chance of making sure we don't wander around unnecessarily. We should camp out here tonight, and start again in the morning. Are you okay with that?"

Eileen didn't say anything. She just looked down at the ground, and then up, facing the road they had in front of them. "I don't know what to say," she said, unsure of herself. "I know that I owe you my life. I can see that you have taken responsibility for me. I don't know how to thank you. So, if that is what you think we should do, let's do that. Are you planning to sleep in the van?"

"Oh no ... No, not in the van. It's a mobile morgue now, you see," Jeff said with a quick laugh, surprised at himself, that he could find even a bit of humour. "No one would want to sleep in that. No one wants to sleep with the dead. And another thing, leaving the body outside the van overnight would not be safe either, if predators should come."

He could not remember when he had last let his humour show. He had had a good sense of it when Faye was still alive, but had lost most of it when she died. Now, out here in the wilderness, with a dead body in a van, and a woman he had saved, he realized he had gotten some of it back. It was strange how, feeling he was doing something worthwhile, and being needed by a helpless human being, had given him back a bit of his spark.

Jeff continued. "I have camped out often in places like this, when I was still in my teens. We can do this. I will spread out my sleeping bag, make it comfortable, and build a good fire, and then we will eat something and then go to sleep. Since I have only one sleeping bag, I will give it to you and you can crawl into that. I will put on my winter coat again and be fine, if I sleep close to the fire. Plus, I have my dogs. They will sleep with me, keeping me warm. We will be fine," Jeff assured her.

"What about tomorrow and the trip to your truck? And what about Bob?" Eileen asked, nodding her head toward the van.

"I will take care of him. You can rest assured of that. I will bring him to town, to the police station, one way or another." Jeff spoke as if there was nothing to worry about but, in the back of his mind, he was not so sure how that would all work out—when he delivered the dead man to the police. The thought of him having killed a man weighed heavily on his mind again, at that moment. But now he had to focus on more pressing matters.

"Here, let me just get this van off the road, in case someone should come by, which I strongly doubt. Leaving it on the road after dark might not be a good idea. It would be good if someone did come by and give us a lift, but I don't see it happening out here, at this time of year. After I get the van off the road I'll get some firewood, and we will build ourselves a good fire." Eileen watched Jeff as he got into the van and drove it toward the side of the road, far enough to let traffic by if anyone should come that way.

Jeff got out of the van and walked toward the hill, a short distance away, to some trees and underbrush. He started picking up pieces of branches that were lying under some of the trees, and some dead twigs. Some of the dead tree branches were quite large in size. With his strong arms he broke a few into some shorter lengths and carried them back to where Eileen was standing close to the van, off the road.

"Here, let me get a fire started and, as soon as it is going, I will get enough wood to last us through the night." Eileen seemed to watch in fascination as Jeff searched out a bare spot of ground, and carefully laid together some large pieces of wood in a criss-cross fashion. He built it up like a little pyramid. Next, into the middle of that little pyramid, he put some small twigs, and bits of dry leaves, and then lit it with a match. In a matter of minutes, a fire was going, and was growing larger by the minute.

"Eileen," he spoke again. "Can you make sure the fire keeps going while I go to get more wood? I think there are some dead trees over there." He was pointing down toward the valley, below them in the west.

"Okay," she responded. "I will try, but what do I do? The fire is going now, is it not?" She didn't sound very confident, or knowledgeable about fire out in the wild.

Jeff realized that Eileen was a city girl, with no outdoor or country experience. If she was to do anything, he would have to show her. She was a college-educated professional who knew about real-estate, money, and city life but not how to survive in the wild. Presently, he spoke up. "Here, look, just keep these pieces of wood in the fire, like so." He bent close to the fire and showed her how to arrange the burning sticks as they got shorter. They would need to be pushed in once they burned down, so they would remain close together and burn better. He straightened up, turned, and left her, walking off toward some trees in the distance, which looked like they held significant amounts of dry wood. After a while, he was back with a huge armful of long sticks—some more like small logs. He made a few repeat trips and had a fairly large supply of wood. "There," he commented. "That will last us through the night. Now, let's get something to eat, something to drink, and we'll rest."

"I don't like the idea of spending another night out here in the wild, but at least I'm not spending it with that killer," Eileen commented, as Jeff got up from the fire and turned toward the van. He was going to look through his back pack and get some of the meat and corn he had packed that morning, and also get something for the dogs.

When Eileen spoke, he stopped momentarily and looked back at her, as she sat on the ground by the fire, bent forward with her hands clasped around her knees. Her hair was still a mess, and it was obvious that in the last few days she had not taken care of herself. But then, how could she, being destined to die at the brutal hands of a serial killer? Her light winter jacket, and her sweater and pants, still had the blood stains she had received when Bob had hit her. Jeff's heart went out to her as he observed her in the gathering shadows of the late afternoon. He wondered, in his heart, what stories lay buried in the soul of this young woman who, as far as he knew, hated men, and had vowed never to see another man if she got out of this situation.

"I will get us something to eat," Jeff said presently, interrupting both of their thoughts, and turned again and continued toward the van. "We need to get some calories into our bodies to keep our strength up. We don't know how much farther we have to go to get to my truck. Even though I am pretty sure we are not too far, we can't take chances. Let me get something together and we will eat."

Jeff walked over to the side door of the van and slid it open. He tried not to notice the silhouette of the body lying under the rug. Reaching behind the driver's seat, he felt for his hunting bag, which lay against the far side. Some of the stuff had been scattered on the floor, when Bob had rummaged through his stuff. He had to get partway into the van to retrieve his pack and the scattered items. Grabbing his 30-06, which lay beside his sleeping bag, he picked up his things and decided that this would be all they would need for the night. He walked back to the fire and set his gear down beside Eileen.

The dogs were lying contentedly near the fire, relaxing lazily in the warmth of the glow. When Jeff returned, they raised their heads, but lay down again as if this was home, and they didn't have a care in the world.

When Jeff set his stuff down, the sight of the gun startled Eileen. Jeff immediately noticed it. "Oh, I'm sorry," Jeff said. "I just brought this along in case we might get company. Hope not to have to use it, of course. Unless we see a deer tomorrow before we get to the truck, that is. But I doubt that."

Jeff proceeded to sort through his stuff, getting out the small, lightweight aluminium cookware, and some of the canned meat. He opened a can of meat and dumped the contents into the tiny pan. Next he took a piece of stick and dug around in the fire, removing several glowing chunks of burning charcoal, and bringing them together outside the fire. He arranged the glowing pieces in such a way that he could set the little pan on some pieces of wood with the glowing coals between them.

"There," he said. "That will do for heating up this meat." He put the meat in the pan carefully set the small pan on the glowing embers of wood. Almost immediately the meat began to sizzle in the pan. "We'll just warm this up good before we eat it. It doesn't really have to cook," Jeff commented, speaking to no one in particular. Next, he picked up one of the cans of dog food, and held it up for his dogs to see. "Brick, Max ... see this? This is for you," he commented again. "Here, let's find something to put this on." Jeff looked around, seeing if he could find something to put the food on. "Wait, I got an idea," he said, getting up and walking over to the van. Once at the van, he opened the driver's side door and grabbed the floor mat. "Here, this will work," he said, returning to the fire, and the food he was warming up. He turned the mat upside down with the rubber side up and spread it out for the dogs. Next, he dumped the dog food on the mat, and the dogs dug in heartily, wolfing down the chunks of meat. Then, Jeff took two of the water bottles from his bag and handed one to Eileen. He sat next to his little charcoal fire keeping watch over the pan of sizzling beef spam. He decided that it would be good to have something else besides just this spam. Jeff took a can of corn, opened it with the can opener on his Leatherman tool, and dumped the contents into the pan alongside the meat.

As the food was warming up, Jeff kept his eyes focused on the task at hand. But his mind wandered occasionally to Eileen. He wondered again what lonely life this poor young woman must have led. He also wondered if she was wondering about him. "I would wonder about someone who had rescued me," Jeff thought, as he refocused on his task at hand.

The meat and corn were hot, and Jeff spooned some onto a small plate and handed it to Eileen. "Here, try this," he said. "I'm sorry that it's not much, but I'm not much of a cook, you see. Just me and my dogs. We live by ourselves and don't spend a lot of time around food, I guess. We eat a lot of prepared and canned stuff." Eileen's quick glance up at him made him catch his thoughts. He realized he had said something that caught her attention. But she didn't speak.

Eileen took the plate. "Thank you," she said. "Don't apologize for your cooking. I have had almost nothing to eat since I was abducted. I only got a little bit of food and water, here and there." She took the plate and, with a fork, began eating.

Jeff wondered what that glance she had given him had been about. In his mind, he shrugged it off. "Maybe it was nothing," he thought. He helped himself to some of the meat and corn, and took the small plate on his lap as he sat cross-legged on the ground. Picking up the little aluminium plate of food, he paused. He always gave a prayer of thanks for his food before he ate. Would Eileen understand? He had suddenly remembered the earlier outburst she had given when he had referred to matters of faith and belief in God.

Eileen sensed his pause. "Is something wrong?"

"No, no." Jeff said, "I always pray before my meals, and I know that you think differently than I do about prayer. I don't mean to offend you, but I always thank God for the food that I have been blessed with." He waited for her response.

"What can I say?" Eileen said, and shrugged. "I don't agree with your religion, but if it works for you, go ahead. It won't bother me."

Jeff bowed his head and gave thanks for the food and asked a blessing on it. He proceeded to eat his heated-up spam and corn. It was good. He had not eaten all day and this was good for his stomach.

As he was finishing his plate, he realized that Eileen was not eating, and was looking at him. It made him feel awkward. He didn't know if he should say something, or what he should do. He pretended not to notice, and diverted his mind to the fire, deciding to rearrange the logs.

Eileen spoke. "When you gave me the food, you said something about not being much of a cook, and that it was just you and the dogs. Do you live alone?"

"Yes, it's just me and my dogs," Jeff responded.

Right now, Jeff didn't feel like doing any more talking, especially about his personal life. He was tired out by all that he had been through. He figured it would be best to continue talking some other time, and in a different setting.

"Eileen," Jeff began, "I think it would be good to bed down for the night and get some rest. This fire is going well, and I will keep putting wood on it through the night. But for now, let's just focus on getting some much-needed rest. Are you okay with that?"

Eileen nodded. She was exhausted from the last few days. Getting rest sounded good. "I'm okay with that."

Jeff got up and prepared to arrange the campsite for the night. The dogs had already gotten comfortable close to the fire, and were snoozing restfully. He got his sleeping bag and spread it out next to Eileen, where she was sitting.

"Here, this should do you," Jeff commented, as he spread the sleeping bag out a little ways away from the fire. He was careful not to put it so close that sparks would drift over to the sleeping bag and set it on fire, and not so far away that the warmth of the fire would not reach her. "Just crawl into this thing and you will be fine till morning. It is heavily insulated and would keep you warm in below-freezing temperatures," Jeff commented. "I think, in the morning, we will get up early ... as soon as it is daylight, and begin our walk. We will make it," he finished, reassuringly.

Jeff walked over to the other side of the fire, put some more pieces of wood on it and arranging them in a way that they would burn slowly, but not so slowly that they would die. Then he scraped a small spot clean from small rocks, and debris, and lay down by his dogs. They seemed to enjoy having their master right next to them as they settled for the night.

Chapter 7

Jeff didn't fall asleep for a long time, even though he had his eyes closed. His mind was restless and, at the same time, afraid about the experience that he had been through, and what the fallout of that would be.

After a while, he opened his eyes, looking at Eileen, in the glow of the flames and saw that she was out, breathing steady and evenly. "Poor woman," Jeff thought. "I wonder what would have happened to her by now, had I not come upon the scene." He knew in his heart that he had done the right thing in rescuing her, but it had been a close call. He shuddered, even now, to think of how close he had been to getting killed himself. In his heart, he thanked God for allowing him to live and experience another day. He started getting drowsy and, after a while, was asleep.

Jeff woke up every few hours during the night, checking the fire each time, and putting fresh pieces of wood on it. It continued to burn through the long dark hours. The temperature sank below freezing, but it was warm in the vicinity of the fire. The dogs lay contentedly next to Jeff, as if this was home.

Toward morning, when dawn began to break, Jeff got up, stretched and put a few more pieces of wood on the fire. Looking over to where Eileen was sleeping, he could see that she was still completely out. She was just as she had been when she had fallen asleep the evening before, and had not stirred. Jeff sat for a while, looking into the fire and thinking about the steps ahead, and about her. He wondered what this day would bring, and what he would face when he got back to town, and to his community.

Jeff sat for a while, meditating and thinking about his situation. Then he got up and walked around the fire, close to Eileen. He crouched down close beside her and spoke gently. "Eileen, it's getting on toward morning. We need to be getting ready to move on." She didn't stir at first but then, slowly, began moving. In an instant, she was wide awake, looking bewildered and unsure of where she was. In a moment, it all came back to her. She crawled out of the sleeping bag, and looked around, scanning the area. Next, she looked up at Jeff, still crouching between her and the fire.

"Good morning, Eileen," Jeff greeted her. "Did you sleep well?"

"I, uh ... yeah, I guess so."

"You slept like a rock, after you lay down. I was awake for a bit yet, but you were out."

"I don't remember falling asleep," 'Eileen commented. "I remember crawling into the sleeping bag ... thinking, 'at least I'm safe now.' That was the last thing I remember."

Jeff took that comment as a compliment. It meant a lot to him to hear a woman say she felt safe with him, as a single man, and a widower, who was not sure anymore where he fit in society.

"Well, let's eat something, and get moving," Jeff said. "We need to get going. I don't want to remain out here any longer than we have to."

"How far do you think it is to your truck?" Eileen questioned. "Do you think we may be close?"

"Yes, I do, out there somewhere." Jeff motioned with his hand toward the hills in the distance. "It's supposed to be over this ridge. I know we have not passed it, I just don't know how much father it is to get there. But first, let's eat." Jeff reached over to his pack and picked out some more canned meat, and a tin of corn. "Here, let's eat this. It's the same as we had last night, unfortunately." He reached in and grabbed another can of dog food.

The dogs had not stirred till now, as if they were not sure they wanted to get up just yet from their warm bed near the fire. Jeff opened the dog food and dumped it on the mat where he had put last evening's food. In an instant, the dogs were up and by the mat, swallowing their canned food with huge bites.

After feeding the hungry dogs, Jeff took the dishes he had used last night, and dumped the canned meat and corn into the dishes. The night before, he had taken a bit of water from one of the bottles and given the dishes a rinse. He repeated the same procedure he had used the night before when he made supper, again prodding some red hot coals toward the outside of the fire and setting the small pan on the coals. In minutes the food was hot and he put some into a plate and handed it to Eileen. Next he put some into his own plate, sat down cross-legged and picked up his fork to eat. He lifted the plate to face level and, this time looking upward, gave a one sentence thanks toward God.

Eileen had observed what he did. She didn't speak as she began to eat. After a few minutes, Jeff spoke again. "Okay," he began, "let's clean up here as soon as we're done. We have to get going and get to my truck as soon as we can. I guess we'll have to carry the most important stuff, and the rest we will have to leave here." Jeff focused his attention on eating for a while, and then spoke up again. "I think I got it. I was going to use the dogs to carry the venison, if I shot a deer, but I guess that will not be necessary now. So, they can carry the stuff. I know that yesterday I carried the stuff, but today will be different" Eileen was listening the whole time Jeff was speaking, even though he seemed to be doing so to no one in particular. Jeff looked at his dogs, as if to size them up. "Max and Brick, come here," Jeff said, crouching down. "I will need you to do some hard work for me. Can you do it?" The dogs were looking at him together, as if waiting for him to give orders.

Jeff got up, went to his stuff and got his long, sharp hunting knife. "I will need to make a travois," he said.

"You're going to need to make a 'what'?" Eileen asked, speaking up after a lengthy silence.

"A Travois," Jeff said again.

"What is a travois?"

"It's a device that was used by natives years ago, to drag loads. If you look in some old books you may see pictures of natives dragging loads behind horses, or dogs, on a contraption of sticks. Usually a travois consists of two sticks side by side, a few feet apart at one end, and closer together toward the other, held together with cross-members. On top of that stretcher-like thing, a load is placed and the travois is hitched to a horse, or a dog. You'll see as soon as I have it completed," Jeff replied.

Jeff got his large, heavy knife and walked over to some tall, thin poplar trees nearby. Picking out two that were thick enough to carry a heavy load, but not too thick for him to notch, and break off, he got to work with his long, wide and heavy-bladed knife. With swift, sharp hacking motions he cut notches into two of the small trunks, close to the bottom. He notched the first one and leaned his body against it. It cracked. Giving it a strong push with his body, it broke off at the notched area. Then he repeated the same thing with the other small tree. The trees were thick and long enough to suit his needs. Next, he took his sharp knife and notched some heavy branches from another tree nearby. He would use these as cross-members. Then he dragged his trees and branches back to the campsite.

He took the knife and lopped off the smaller branches. In a short while, the trunks were clean. Next, he reached into his bag and grabbed some rope, cutting off a few, two-foot-long lengths of it. He unravelled and undid the strands and made three cords out of each piece of rope he had cut. Then, he laid out the trees in stretcher form, putting the wide end of the trunks at one end and the thin ends at the other. He tapered the contraption from two-feet-wide at the heavy end, to about one-foot-wide at the top, using the smaller branches as cross-members to create something of a bed.

"What is it supposed to do?" Eileen asked, watching Jeff intently. It was obvious that she was fascinated by what Jeff was doing. She was not used to improvising anything. Having grown up in the city, everything in her life had, at least, an instruction manual. She commented again. "You don't need that large of a contraption to carry this little bit of stuff, do you?"

"No, the travois is not for our stuff, at least not all of it," Jeff responded, focusing on getting his ropes ready and laying them out where he would use them to tie the wood together. "This travois is for the body in the van."

Eileen started, but she said nothing. Jeff noticed it. "I can't leave the body out here. It's too big of a chance to take. Who knows what could happen to it? If we walk away from here, and leave it, and someone finds it, it could cause problems. And I would have to explain what happened. It will be hard enough as it is, to explain everything, and I don't want to lose the body. I need to get the body to town as soon as possible."

"But this contraption you are putting together here ... do you think the dogs can drag it with the body on it?" Eileen asked. "I would just leave the body here or, if you think you have to do something, hide the body until you get to town and report what happened, and then come back with the police and get it."

Jeff seemed impatient now. "You are right Eileen, that would be a possibility, and I have thought about it. The risk, however, is too much; I don't want to take it. Besides, what if we get snow? And if we should get a heavy snow, who knows how soon we would be able to get back here? Also, as soon as the news is out that you have been rescued, the media will be all over you, and me too perhaps, and we will be questioned relentlessly. No. I want to take the body now." Jeff finished his sentence as if it was final.

Eileen made no response for a while. "Is there anything you need me to do?"

"Sure, if you want to get all of the things together and stuff it into the bag, that would be good." Jeff said, picking up several water bottles and putting them into his oversized coat pockets. "We will need these," he mentioned.

Jeff focused his attention again on the task at hand, getting the dogs to pull the travois. "With the dogs dragging the travois, I think we can take it all with us. When you put the stuff in the bags, take the guns from the van and put them in the bag too. We can't leave them here. The police will want the guns. Just make sure you leave my gun where it is. I will carry it. We won't be shooting deer, but I want it with me just the same."

The mention of the guns unsettled Eileen's mind, but she tried not to show it. As much as she didn't understand, or know this man Jeff, she knew her safety still very much depended on him. If he should decide to abandon her now, she would still be hopelessly lost and, most likely, die out here in the elements.

Jeff was finishing tying the last of the pieces of wood on the travois, making it a sturdy structure. This travois had to be a bit different than he remembered seeing in books, because he needed it to be dragged between the dogs, and not just behind one. And he could not have the dogs in single file. To accommodate that, he put a pole across the front end of the travois to make some form of cross bar, kind of a yoke which he would lay across the shoulders of the dogs. He wrapped some of the wrapping cloth around the piece of wood, making it look rather large and bulky. With the cross-member wrapped up like that, at least the dogs backs would not be rubbed raw by the wooden pole. Next, he called the dogs. Max and Brick came up to Jeff, and he began talking to them.

The travois only needed to carry a fairly lightweight body, over what Jeff believed would be about one to two hours of walking. On the backs of the dogs, that weight was only a fraction of the total weight, given that the end dragging on the ground carried the greater part of the load. Jeff explained to his dogs what he was planning to do. "Look boys, the body inside the van will be put on this contraption and you will have to drag it for who knows how many kilometres. Here, come let's put on your saddlebags and attach them to this cross-member." Jeff got the saddlebags and harnessed the dogs. They were used to the bags and didn't mind them. But when Jeff laid the lightweight contraption on their shoulders, the dogs were confused. "It's okay boys, don't worry about. Take it easy and it will all be good," Jeff continued.

After he got the dogs harnessed, he walked over to the van and proceeded to get the body out of the van, making sure that he would not dislodge the blanket in which the corpse was wrapped. By now, the body was stiff as a log, which Jeff figured would help in tying it down on the travois. He carried the body over to the travois, and laid it on the bottom end, with the feet toward the dogs, and the head down, to keep the weight off the dogs. Then he took some more rope and tied the body down so it would not roll and fall off.

Eileen was ready with the bag of gear. "Do you have the guns in there?" Jeff asked. She nodded. Jeff picked up his 30-06, and slung it over his shoulder. "Okay, let's go. Max, Brick, follow me," Jeff spoke to the dogs. Jeff picked up the bag of gear and began walking upward toward the ridge of the hill. The dogs pulled on the travois, but Jeff sensed that this was perhaps a bit much for his dogs, not being used to carrying or pulling heavy loads like this. They would need help. "Okay, you can do it boys, come on. Pull!" Jeff coaxed the dogs. The dogs pulled together and this time they began moving. It was clear that it would be tough going. Jeff paused and mentally figured what would be the best way of getting to his truck with the least amount of difficulty. The terrain was somewhat grassy, just like it had been yesterday when he stumbled upon the crime scene. But there were some rocky spots, with trees as well. He decided that instead of straight up the hill, he would go up the hill at an angle, to make the ascent less difficult for the dogs, and also for himself and Eileen.

"Let's go boys, let's go." Jeff coaxed the dogs onward again. The dogs were struggling with the load, but they were moving. Jeff stopped the team, and made a decision. Eileen saw that he was up to something. "What are you planning now?" she asked. Jeff didn't speak, but just put the bag of stuff down on the travois, on top of the low end of the body, and quickly tied it down. Next, he took a lengthy piece of rope, made a quick double loop, and slid it over his head, onto his right shoulder, and under his left arm, and tied it to the travois between the dogs. With his thick winter coat, he would have a good pad to protect him from the rope rubbing against him.

"Let's go boys," Jeff coaxed the dogs again. Now, with Jeff's added strength on the travois, pulling not only forward but also up, the dogs were easily able to pull the load. Jeff made for the hill at an angle and walked with a brisk step. Eileen had to struggle just to keep up with him. "Why are you going so fast?" she asked.

"Oh, sorry. I wasn't thinking." Jeff said. "I guess we can go slower. Let's just walk steady upward, and toward that ridge. Once we are on top, going down the other side will be a lot less difficult. Then the dogs will be able to do it no problem."

For the next half hour, neither Jeff nor Eileen spoke. Eileen tried her best to keep up. The steady fast-paced walking was a struggle, but she managed. She observed this man Jeff, as he led the way. He continued to amaze her. She saw that he was resolute, firm and yet ever so gentle. As she was walking behind the travois, her mind went back to how he had rescued her. While her feet carried her along the path the travois made, her mind carried her back to the night before. She remembered telling him in the van that she never wanted to see another man. She wondered why she had said that. Were there perhaps still men in this world who were gentle, thoughtful and trustworthy?' She remembered her mother and her struggles as a single parent raising her, and how difficult it had been for her mother to provide for herself as a working mother with a child. It seemed men had just taken advantage of her mother. And now she had almost gotten killed by a murderer. As she thought about the last few days, her mind went to the killer that Jeff had killed. Jeff truly had been her rescuer. In her heart, she wondered what it was that made Jeff the way he was. How could men be so different? One man a ruthless creature, worse than a wild animal and, the other, a person who's mission, it seemed, was to help people who could not help themselves.'

Jeff's voice cut into her thoughts. "Okay, we have reached the top." It was a good while since they had started plodding uphill at an angle. The climb had been much longer and farther up than Jeff had imagined. Apparently, they were not nearly at the right place, the hilltop beyond which the truck would be waiting. Farther south, the hill would narrow down to a small ridge, but this far north it was still a large hill. Just the same, Jeff wanted to get down to the other side and to the road as soon as possible. Jeff continued. "I would like for us, now, to go straight down. I don't want us to go too far south, in case we miss the spot where I have the truck," Jeff commented. "But first, let's stop for a bit of a breather." Eileen was glad for that. Jeff searched out a spot, not too rough, and sat down. "Let's get something to drink." Jeff said, reaching into his coat pocket and getting out two water bottles. He handed one to Eileen, and she accepted it gratefully. Even though it was a cold day, and the temperatures were around freezing, with the morning fire, and the hot food, and now with this exercise, it had not been too cold yet. If only they could reach the bottom of this hill, and reach the road that ran parallel with it, they could reach the pickup truck with no problems.

After fifteen minutes of rest, Jeff spoke up again. "Okay, let's go." Eileen got up and was ready, together with Jeff. He led the way, with the dogs following. Now, it was an easy job, walking downhill. The dogs sensed it too, that their load had gotten a lot lighter to pull. After a while of walking down hill, Jeff spoke up. "There it is, see?" he pointed into the distance. Eileen looked up and saw a winding gravel road in the distance, through some trees. When they got to the road, Jeff looked in both directions, as if to decide which direction would lead toward his truck, and then walked to the side of the road and decided to sit again for a few minutes. "Let's take another break. We need to conserve our strength. No need to overdo it this close to the end of our walk." Jeff sat down, took out his water bottle, and finished the last of it.

"How are you making out, Eileen?" Jeff asked. "Are you doing okay?"

"I'm tired, and I have pain from my injuries, but other than that it's fine."

"Good," Jeff commented. "I think you have done well, given that this is not your regular life-style."

"I would have never dreamed that places like this even exist," she said. "This is a different world out here, for sure. If I had gotten to know this part of the world in a different set of circumstances, I might even like it."

Jeff's heart skipped a beat. "This city girl," he thought, "college trained and completely urbanized, making this kind of comment, says more about her inner person than she probably realizes. Who knew what inner longings lay dormant in her soul, never having been exposed to the sunlight of life. What if her heart could be drawn into the light and exposed to the warmth of true humanity. What could she become?" Jeff dismissed his thoughts. His first priority right now was getting Eileen, the dogs, himself, and the body to the truck.

"We need to get moving again." Jeff said. "I just hope the truck is not too far away, anymore. Okay, Max and Brick, time to move again." Jeff picked up his part of the harness and put it over his right shoulder and under his left shoulder again. The dogs faithfully pulled their share of the load, together with their master. Now, with the hard surface of the road under them, the travois moved rather easily. Jeff walked at a steady pace, keeping a strong stride.

For Eileen, it was again all she could do to keep up. But she was determined that she would not complain. She would do her best. After another forty minutes of walking, Jeff stopped. "Time to take a break again," he said. "I thought we should be at the truck by now. It can't be too much father." He sat down beside the road, and the dogs lay down right under their harness, just the way they had stopped. Jeff realized that the dogs were getting tired. As good and as strong and healthy as they were, this was an unusual load for them. Jeff got up, walked over to his hunting bag, undid it from its ropes and reached inside, getting out several more water bottles. He handed one to Eileen, and took the other for himself. He took the dish he had cooked breakfast in and dumped two bottles of water into it and set it before the dogs. They heartily lapped up the water. That would have to do till evening, by which time he hoped they would be back in town.

It took another few hours of steady walking before the two weary people, with the dogs and the body on the travois, reached the spot where the pickup was parked. It was just the way Jeff had left it the morning before. "We're here," Jeff said excitedly. "Eileen, here are the keys, unlock it, get the stuff in, and start it up while I get the dogs unhitched, and put this body in the back of the truck." Eileen needed no prodding. While Jeff quickly undid the ropes from the dogs harnesses, Eileen quickly unlocked the truck and started the motor. Next, she grabbed the bag of gear, and Jeff's rifle and stowed it in the back. She opened the door for the dogs to jump in, and they knew without being told what they were to do. Jeff picked up the stiff, wrapped body and put it on the bed of the truck. Next, he jumped in the driver's seat and, with Eileen in the passenger seat and the dogs in the back, he turned the truck around and headed south, down the gravel road and back toward civilization.

"Some deer hunting trip this had turned out to be," Jeff thought to himself. Now he needed to focus on how he was going to deal the situation he had before him. He was aware that part of him was still numb from the whole experience. Later, he would feel it more. But for the next few hours, he would concentrate on driving.

Chapter 8

Jeff guided his trusted dodge pickup back the way he had come the previous morning. Even though the ride back was only a matter of hours, it seemed long. As he was driving, it was getting toward noon when Jeff decided to try his cell phone to see if he had service. He reached for his phone and flipped it open. Sure enough, there were a few bars, indicating he was within reach of a cell phone tower.

"Eileen, I have to call the police station and let them know you have been found, plus tell them all the other stuff that has happened. Is there anything you want me to say to them?"

"No, just do what you got to do. I am just looking forward to going back to Ruby Miller's place and getting showered and go to sleep for a week."

Jeff dialled 911, and listened for the other end to respond.

"Emergency," came the reply on the other end.

Jeff was not used to making 911 calls, and was not sure what to say, but he began anyway. "I have some important news. The woman named Eileen Benson that was missing a few days ago, I have found her. She is alive, and is with me in my truck. I am bringing her to town."

"What is your name?"

"Jeff Nolan," Jeff responded. He wondered why he had not thought of stating his name right away.

"Where are you now, Jeff?" the voice from the other end came again.

"I'm coming south on County Rd 35, about an hour or so away from Forest Hill."

"Is Miss Benson okay?"

"She is doing fine considering her circumstances," he responded. "But she will need to be seen by a doctor. She has been through a rough ordeal."

"Okay, bring her to the emergency and there will be police and doctors waiting for you."

When he heard the word *police* his mind jolted a bit. He knew that this was going to happen, but it was going to be soon now, and there was no way he could mentally prepare himself for this in a way that calmed him down. He was very nervous about how this whole thing would play itself out. And that was not all. He had some more news that would only add to the story. He had to tell the person at the other end of the line more.

"I have something else as well," Jeff continued. "I have her abductor with me too, but he's dead." Jeff noticed silence on the other end of the line after he spoke that sentence.

After a few seconds the voice came back on the line. "What did you say?"

"I got the man who abducted her in the back of my truck, and he is dead," Jeff repeated.

"Let me transfer you," the female voice responded. "Hold the line."

"Hello, Constable Gray speaking, what is this you mentioned about a dead man with you?"

Jeff paused a moment. "I have the abductor with me in the back of my truck. He is dead. I will explain it as soon as I get the woman to the hospital."

"Where are you now?"

"I'm about an hour or so away from Forest Hill, coming down County Rd 35."

"What kind of vehicle are you driving?"

Jeff didn't answer right away. "What an awful lot of questions," he thought. "is this just the beginning?' He responded. "I'm driving a brown 2001 dodge 4x4 pickup truck."

"Can you give me your plate number, and your birthday?"

Jeff gave it to him.

"We will keep an eye out for you, just come to the emergency, and we will talk there," the voice at the other end said, and the phone went dead.

Jeff looked at his cell phone. That interchange had lasted only a few minutes. He just hoped that this was not the beginning of a long, living nightmare. In his heart, he knew he had done, and was doing, the right thing. What he was not sure of, was if his story would sell. Would the law believe him? The only way to know was to find out.

Jeff had not been driving more than fifteen or twenty minutes after his phone call when he noticed a police cruiser in his rear view mirror, about two hundred feet behind him. The cruiser was just following him. Again, Jeff wondered how this mess would unfold and what would be required of him. No doubt, this story would end up in the paper. He didn't care for that. But now that he was in it, he would just have to go through with it.

At the little hospital at Forest Hill, Jeff noticed a police cruiser parked by the emergency door. Jeff pulled into the emergency area and parked the truck. The police cruiser that had followed him stopped behind him and a middle-aged officer got out. At the same time, an officer got out of the cruiser that had already been parked there when he arrived.

Jeff walked toward the officer, who had followed him in his cruiser, and began to speak. "Officer, I'm Jeff Nolan. In the truck I have Miss Eileen Benson, the woman who was abducted, and she is in need of medical attention." While Jeff was talking to the officer, the hospital's emergency door opened and a doctor and nurse came out, pushing a wheelchair.

"Is this the truck that brought in Miss Eileen Benson?" the nurse asked.

Jeff turned toward the medical staff, and responded. "Yes, she is in the cab of his pickup truck in the front." He proceeded to go around the cab and opened the door for Eileen and, in the process, walked away from the officer he had just started talking to. This was not Jeff's style or way. He was not used to being important, to being the centre of attention with the focus on him.

Jeff opened the passenger door. "Here, Eileen, let me help you," he said. Without thinking what he was doing, he reached for her hand and gave her assistance in stepping out of his truck.

The doctor reached for Eileen's other hand and, with one look at her, proceeded to set her down in the wheelchair. Jeff looked at Eileen and smiled, "Okay Eileen, I'm glad we got you to safety. Let me know if there is anything I can do for you, okay?" Eileen's one eye was still quite bruised and a bit swollen, but both eyes were watery as she simply nodded. The nurse turned the wheelchair and wheeled Eileen into the hospital.

Jeff turned back to the officer who had followed him to the passenger side of the truck, with a note-pad in his hand, getting ready to ask him some questions. By now the other officer had joined his partner. Jeff motioned to the back of his truck. "Underneath this blanket is the body of the dead man, the kidnapper," Jeff said.

"Let me see," the middle-aged officer said. He walked to the truck, looked at the wrapped-up blanket and pulled a bit on it, trying to lift up a corner.

"Let me undo some of these ropes," Jeff said. "I tied them up good when I wrapped him up for transportation."

Jeff undid a few of the end ropes at the head of the body, toward the rear end of the truck at the tail gate. The officer pulled back the blanket and, with one look, he was satisfied that there was, indeed, a man in that blanket. He reached for his radio and spoke into it, calling for a coroner..

"Mr. Nolan," the office began, "you will have to come with us and answer some questions, and make a statement."

Jeff had expected this. His mind was trying hard to absorb what was happening. Where would this lead? He just hoped that he would come out clean on the other end. "Okay," he responded.

"Do you have a weapon or weapons on you, or in the truck?" the officer asked.

"I have no weapon on me, but there are several firearms in the truck."

"What is in the truck?" the officer questioned.

"In the truck there is a 30-06, which is mine. Then there is a 12 gauge shotgun, and a hand gun, both belonging to the dead man. At least, they were in his possession early yesterday."

"Okay, Mr. Nolan," the officer said. "Thank you for your information. For now, leave your truck with us. We will take care of it and what is in it. Just leave the keys in it and come with us."

"What about my dogs?" Jeff asked.

The dogs had stayed in the truck because Jeff had told them to, but they were eagerly waiting to be allowed out of the truck, and freedom to roam.

"You will have to have them on a leash, and then you can take them with you. They will have to ride in the back seat beside you."

"Okay, good," Jeff responded. Jeff got two leashes from his truck, put them on his dogs and together with them was escorted to the cruiser and into the back seat. They needed no prompting. They obediently hopped in the back seat. The plexiglass wall between the front and back seats of the cruiser would protect the officer if there was any danger to him from the dogs.

Jeff was silent as the officer got into the front and they left the hospital parking lot, heading toward the station. It was only a few blocks to the station but, again, enough for Jeff to wonder where this journey would take him. Would he be prosecuted? Would he be charged? Who knew what lay ahead? At the station, he was told to just leave the dogs in the cruiser, for the moment. Jeff didn't think it wise to leave the dogs in the cruiser given that they had been in the truck for several hours, and not knowing how long the questioning would take. Upon request he was allowed to take them for a brief exercise period to run around and relieve themselves, but then he had to put them into the back of the police car again. Jeff was escorted into a small room where an officer in a white shirt and black tie was waiting for him.

"Hi, I'm detective Evans," he introduced himself. "Tell me who you are, what you were doing, what happened, and so on."

Inwardly Jeff groaned. Telling this story was going to be a difficult task. Jeff sat up straight and began from where he had gone hunting and how he had heard the scream and stumbled upon the crime scene. He told the officer how he had tried to find a way not to hurt anyone, but had in the end been left no option but to kill the abductor if he was going to save himself and Eileen.

Almost an hour later, Detective Evans looked up from his stack of hand-written notes. "You have told an incredible story, Jeff. I don't know what will happen, but you will be asked to come in for questioning and perhaps fill in missing gaps. And we will need your help pointing us to the place where you said he wanted to take you. In the meantime, we will run a background check on you to see if you have a clean record, given the fact that you, yourself, said that you killed this abductor. Wait here for a few minutes. I will be back shortly."

Jeff was left alone for a few minutes. He closed his eyes to think. If his life had been hard before, it had just gotten complicated on top of everything. Also, he realized that there were eyes and ears in that room. Everything he had said was recorded. Another thing, he was thinking of his dogs, in the back seat of the police car. It was getting very long.

After a few minutes, Evans came back. "The information so far checks out," he said. "All we have done so far is check what is in the truck. The guns you described were in the truck. We will run tests on them. You will get your gun and your truck and your stuff back, after we send it to forensics, assuming of course that there are no surprises in this investigation. We have time today, and should get much of that work done. Don't worry for now. In the meantime, we know where you live, we have your information. If you need us for anything, or if you remember something you forgot to tell me, just call. We are here to help. Now, one of our officers will give you a ride home. Do you have another vehicle you can use until we are done with the truck?"

"I have ways of getting around. I can do without the truck for a few days. One of my buddies won't mind picking me up for work and such," Jeff responded.

"Okay then, you are free to go," Detective Evans said.

Jeff got up and walked toward the exit door. The same middle-aged officer who had followed him was waiting for him. "I will be giving you a lift home."

Jeff walked ahead toward the waiting cruiser, with his dogs still in the back seat. The office opened the rear door and Jeff got in. His dogs were happy to see him. The twenty-five kilometre ride to his house didn't seem long.

When Jeff was dropped off at his house, he realized he had left his keys with the truck, and his house keys were on there as well. He walked to the back door, got his hidden key, unlocked the door and went inside. The dogs followed him cheerfully. Jeff went and put some wood in the stove and got a fire going. The house needed warming up, in more ways than just one. After the fire was crackling well in the stove, he put on some coffee and walked toward the cupboard, bringing out a can of dog chow.

"Here Max, and Brick, its supper time," Jeff said.

Next Jeff went to his bedroom, grabbed his bathrobe from its hook on the wall, went into the bathroom, and turned on the hot water. For some reason, he had a heavy leaden feeling about life. "I will get me a good hot shower," he thought, "a coffee, a bite to eat, and will have a good night's rest."

After his shower, he put on his bathrobe and sat down, sipped his coffee, slowly ate some snacks and, for a long time, reflected on the last two days. It seemed like a long time ago since yesterday, early morning, when he had left with his dogs on his first solo hunting trip. What a trip it had turned out to be. As he finished his coffee, he remained deep in thought. The fire was beginning to die down. His mind was still up north, out in the wild where he had met a troubled soul who was a stranger to him, but in distress. As the evening wore on he lost track of time as his mind replayed the events. The hunting trip seemed to have done the exact opposite of what he had hoped for. It was getting quite late when he realized his eyes had gotten heavy with sleep.

He went over to the stove, put in another log, closed the door, and walked into his bedroom. Then, he got out of his bathrobe and into bed, pulling the blanket over himself. Every night for four years he had gone to sleep feeling loneliness, and an icy cold in his heart. Today, the cold was different. Faye was not here with him, but it was as if something was stirring which he could not quite get a handle on. He decided it was time to sleep. He would think about this on another day.

Chapter 9

The phone was ringing early on Monday morning, causing Jeff to wake up groggily from his sleep, trying to figure out what was happening. He looked at his night stand clock and saw that it was already past eight. "Oh no," he thought, "I must have forgotten to set the alarm." Before he could reach for his phone, the answering machine kicked in, and a voice came on the answering machine.

"Hello Mr. Nolan. This is Officer Evans calling from Police Headquarters. When you get this message, please call me back as soon as possible." The officer gave his number and hung up.

Jeff was awake in an instant. He sat up in bed and looked at the phone, deciding when to call back. As he looked at the phone, he saw that it, in fact, had two messages. Then it dawned on him. He was supposed to be at work today! It was Monday morning, and he was supposed to be working by now!

He clicked the on button for the answering machine and listened to the first message. It was the foreman from the shop. "Hello, Jeff, it's a quarter past seven on Monday Morning and I have not seen you at work. I figured I should call you. We need your help on the floor. Please call back if you get this message."

The next message was the one Jeff had already heard from the police station. Jeff decided that he was going to call the police station first and see what was up with the case he was involved in, and see if they needed him. Then he would call his foreman at work.

Jeff dialled the number for the police station and waited. The automated system kicked in and Jeff waited for instructions on which numbers to push to get to the right department. For Detective Evans, the automated system told him to press five. He pushed the number and waited for a response on the other end of the line. It came almost instantly. "Evans speaking."

"Hello, Jeff Nolan here. You just called my number a few minutes ago. Sorry that I was not on time to pick up the phone."

"Oh, yes, Mr. Nolan." Evans sounded excited. "We have some important developments in this case. Eileen's abduction is bigger than it looks. We will need you." Jeff's heart sank at the thought of having to be part of this investigation.

"Am I in trouble?" Jeff asked.

"Not at this point," Evans responded. "What we want you to do is come to the police station. We want to go over some information with you. How soon can you get here?"

"I don't know," Jeff responded. "I don't have a vehicle yet, since my truck is still at the police station for forensics."

"Oh yes, of course, of course. We will send someone to pick you up. Can you be ready in half an hour?" Evans asked.

"Sure, I will be ready," Jeff heard himself say. The line went dead. "I better call my foreman and tell him what is going on," he thought.' He dialled the number.

The secretary's voice came on the line. "Carrier Trailers, Linda speaking."

"This is Jeff Nolan. The foreman left a message on my answering machine, I need to talk with him. Can you put me through to the floor?"

"Hold for a moment," Linda said.

The phone went on hold for a few seconds and then his foreman picked up the receiver. "Todd speaking"

"Hi Todd. Sorry I didn't call in this morning. I apologize, but I had a bad problem on the weekend and things didn't go well, and so this morning I didn't even wake up on time." Jeff knew he sounded very confusing. "I should have called, but I just got a call from the police station and I need to be there, and I don't know how soon I will be able to be back, maybe not today at all, or tomorrow. I just can't say."

"What are you talking about?" Todd wanted to know. "Are you in trouble with the law? We are busy and we need all hands on the floor. Did something happen to you, you sick or something?" Jeff could hear Todd's mind was just spinning with questions.

"I wish I was just sick," Jeff responded. "I'm tired, that's true, but it's much deeper than just a simple little matter with the law. I'm surprised you have not heard anything on the news yet. It has to do with the story last week about the missing woman. I can't say much now except that I am not in trouble, but I have some information that they want to know. I need to let you go. I will be at the police station this morning for a while for sure and then, maybe later, I can catch up with you. I will call you in a while." Jeff hung up.

As much as they needed his help on the floor, he was not going to be able to make it, and he had no idea what the police wanted from him. Jeff quickly fed his dogs, knowing that, in a short while, the police car would be there to pick him up.

The police cruiser that came to pick him up was driven by the same officer who had dropped him off the evening before.

"Good morning Mr. Nolan," the officer greeted him. "How are you today?"

"Good, thanks," Jeff responded. The officer opened the front door of the cruiser for him and he got in. This was a surprise for Jeff. Last night, he had been escorted into the back seat.

As the officer guided the car down the driveway and back to town, he began to talk. "The apartment ran some background checks on you last night, and they found nothing. The guns all checked out as well. Nothing wrong there either. What you told us matches. But we are not finished with you yet. We are going to need your support and your help to do some digging. When you told us what this man Bob said to you about other killings he had done, well, we are searching and trying to find some leads. Oh, by the way, the man's name was not Bob. His name is Oscar Ritchie. He lives, or lived rather, about 100 kilometres west of Forest Hill. He owns a small farm, and did some odd jobs on the side, renovation jobs mostly. We have very little history about him. We checked out his dad, a cranky old man. He is still alive, but there's no relationship between the two from the information we have."

"What will you need from me," Jeff wondered aloud.

"We will need to go and do some searching up north, where you told us this took place. The sooner we can get to it the better. This morning there will be a couple of SUVs ready, with forensic specialists, to go up and check out that place. This could be a big break in some long open crime files. We will need you to guide us to that spot."

"Alright, I guess I can do that," Jeff agreed. "I would just like to call my work and let them know I won't be in today."

"Go ahead, call your boss."

Jeff made the call from his cell phone. He informed his boss briefly that there was no chance of him coming in to work that day, as he was needed by the police to do some research work for the day, and so he would not be in. His boss complied. Jeff turned off the phone and rode in silence the rest of the way to the station. At the station, he followed the officer inside and was told to wait in the hallway until forensics got there. At 10 am they were ready. Two 4x4 Chevy SUVs with 4 officers in one, and two in the other, plus Jeff, made a team of seven people.

The leader of the team motioned to Jeff. "Hi Mr. Nolan, my name is Pete. You will ride with me. We will need you to show us the way."

They got underway and, in a short while, they were back on the same stretch of road heading north, where Jeff had gone a few days earlier on his deer hunting trip. Pete, the officer behind the wheel, was a tall lanky officer, early thirties, with an atmosphere of experience and confidence about him.

"So, Mr. Nolan, how far is it?" Pete asked.

"A couple of hours, depending on how you drive, of course," Jeff responded. "It took me several hours to get to the place where I parked my truck, and then I walked over the hill to the place where I was captured. The kidnapper drove another hour and a half or more, but that was slow driving. It was not that it was so much distance, as much as it was slow driving due to the condition of the road. But I don't know how much of a detour we will have to make to come up to the place where the, ah, what's his name ... Oscar, took his vehicle. I am thinking if we take a left where I took a right; it will bring us around the bottom end of the hill, and up the valley on the other side. But I can't be sure of that."

"We will have to try," Pete said calmly.

As they drove, the distance flew by a lot faster in this late model SUV. As they came up to the intersection where Jeff had turned left, Jeff motioned up ahead. "Turn left there." The officer made the turn and the SUV behind them followed. After another short distance, they came to the end of the road where Jeff had taken the right turn. He remembered that he had seen what looked like tire tracks, turning toward the left. "Slow down here." Jeff said. The officer did as Jeff suggested.

"See that?" Jeff said, "There, you see a set of tracks going off to the right. That was my truck on Saturday morning. But look closely toward the left, it looks like there is a trace of tire tracks going that way, toward the left. Can you follow them?"

"Sure, let's follow them." Pete responded.

In another few minutes, just as Jeff had guessed they would, they were coming up around the bottom of the hill and heading in a northerly direction. The road was winding, hugging the hillside. Then Jeff saw it. "Look, there. That is the place where I found the van on Saturday!" Jeff said excitedly, pointing off to the right and little way up the hill.

"Are you sure?" Pete asked.

"I'm sure. I remember because I named those two big pine trees by that rock. I named them *Twin Pines rock* as a reference point to get back to if I got free from him."

Pete pulled the SUV off the road toward the right, and put it in park, letting the motor idle. The SUV behind them did the same. Pete got out and walked over to the driver's side of the vehicle behind them.

He came back and spoke to his fellow officer. "We are going to look around here for a little bit before we go on, to verify some things," he said.

It didn't take long for the officers to determine that there had, in fact, been some activity going on in that area.

They didn't find anything except the remains of a campfire, and some strewn garbage, left over wrappings and so on. The officers took pictures of various spots and picked up anything that looked like it had been handled by human hands.

After a while of scouring the area, the team assembled, put bags of various items into the back of the leading SUV, and got into the vehicles. Jeff was still sitting in the leading SUV. Pete got in behind the wheel. "Jeff, we need you to show us the spot where you told us you overpowered your abductor."

"It's quite a ways up ahead yet. It seemed like a long distance anyway, but I think it was because I was tied up and scared," Jeff said.

"As long as you recognize the place when we get there. That is what is important, at this point," Pete said, with determination.

Rapidly, the two vehicles made their way northward again. Jeff kept his eyes peeled for landmarks, trying to remember what he had seen through front windshield, while sitting in the back of the van, tied up. Again, Jeff was surprised at how fast the SUVs travelled on this road. They were much faster than Oscar's Safari van had been. All of a sudden, Jeff noticed the narrow road off to the left, going down into the valley.

"There, that narrow road to the left, downhill. That's it," Jeff spoke, excitedly. Officer Pete braked sharply, and swerved onto the road leading into the valley below. "Just follow this trail and you will come to somewhat of a clearing, close to the creek." Jeff spoke with confidence. "We are almost there."

As they moved down the hill, Jeff saw the clearing ahead, where Oscar had parked his van, built a fire and almost taken Jeff's his life.

"There, that's it. That is where Oscar took me and Eileen. See that there," Jeff pointed toward the remains of a campfire. "That is where Oscar built a fire on Saturday."

The SUVs stopped, and the officers got out. Pete and his fellow officer walked to the rear vehicle and talked with the other team members. Presently, Pete came back and looked at Jeff. "Mr. Nolan, we will be here for a while. We want you to retrace the steps you took on Saturday, when you said you killed Oscar. We want you to show us what happened, and where you believed he wanted to take you to show you his 'information.' "

"Okay," Jeff responded. "It's this way." Jeff led the way down toward the nearby creek. As he came closer, he point out the tracks in the mud. "See those tracks? I made those. And these here, they belong to Oscar."

One of the officers was holding a camera and was pointing it, shooting pictures of anything that might be of value. He took pictures of the tracks, and then measured the distances between foot steps.

Jeff led the way up to the water and stopped. "Here is where I went into the water, and over there, on that side, you see the foot prints where I stopped, stooped down and grabbed the mud that I threw in Oscar's face. It was at that point that I was able to overpower Oscar and take his shotgun from him."

"This is good so far. Let's go across Jeff, and you can show us the way up the hill," Pete instructed. "Is there a way to get across with out getting our boots full of water?"

Jeff carefully picked his way across the water on some of the larger rocks just below the surface of the water the water. On the other side, he led the way up the incline. After a short distance, Jeff stopped. "About here is where Oscar pulled his gun on me, and where I shot him with his shotgun," Jeff said. "From here on out, I don't know where Oscar would have taken me, except that he pointed up and to the right,"

Pete looked for a moment at the spot where Jeff said Oscar had pulled the gun on him, and where he had shot Oscar.

The other two officers came forward, looking at the ground. They slowly, and carefully, examined it. The dried blood, from Oscar's gunshot wound, was still on the ground.

"Let's pause here for a bit and check this place out," Pete suggested. "We need to make sure we get all the information possible." The two officers worked quickly and thoroughly, photographing the area, the markings on the ground, and taking samples of the dried blood.

After a while, they seemed satisfied and Pete spoke again. "Jeff, let's go up to where you said Oscar had pointed."

They made their way up the hill. It was not long before they came to a bit of a clearing and some, rather large, boulders, which made somewhat of a sheltered area. There was foot print evidence, of former human presence. The officers stopped, examining the area. "I don't see anything here that is of help," Pete mentioned. "We need to keep looking. It looks like this may be a trail that leads us past this area. Why don't we walk past this place a little bit and see where it leads."

Fred, a short stocky officer, had walked ahead for a short distance, where the path came up close against a rock wall. "I think I may have something here."

The rest of the team quickly followed. "Here, I think these rocks have been moved," Pete noticed. In what had looked like a rocky wall, there was evidence that the rocks had been moved at some point.

"Do we have some tools to loosen and move them?" Pete asked.

"I can radio the other guys by the vehicles and tell them bring us some equipment from the truck," Fred answered.

"I think I can move them," Jeff volunteered. "Here, let me try."

"Don't hurt yourself," Pete said, "We can do it with tools if we need to."

Jeff was already by the rock wall, scanning which rock would be a key rock to breaking open the pile. He grabbed one of the top rocks and, with his strong muscular arms, rolled it out, like a soccer ball, and let it roll down past his feet. He pulled another one, and then another. It was evident that this was an entrance of some kind. An opening existed here that lead to some place inside the hill.

"I don't want to go in there," Jeff said, as he pulled a few more large rocks away.

"Don't worry," Pete said with a short laugh. "That's our job. We will take care of that."

Jeff pulled the last rock from what had turned out to be an opening into some sort of cave. Pete got on the radio and asked for assistance. He looked at his short partner, and asked. "Can you get in there, Fred?"

"Sure, I think so." Fred responded, as he got down on his hands and knees, grabbed his flashlight and moved forward. It was a bit like crawling into an igloo on all four. He disappeared into the black hole. In the next moment he called out. "This is a cave all right, and you won't believe what we have here. Get me a camera, more lights and have one of the other guys come in too. There are remains of some bodies here, appearing to be women."

Jeff shuddered. In his mind, he replayed what had happened, and what Oscar had said he was going to show him. Despite all the evil things about Oscar, he had spoken the truth about his intentions. This was the hiding place where Oscar had hidden his victims. No doubt, he would have had him go up that hill, even open up the cave for him, and then have him crawl into the cave before shooting him and hiding him in that cave. Later, he would have done the same with Eileen. This cave was, at least one of, the burial grounds for the other victims he had talked about.

The voice of Pete speaking into the radio brought him back to reality. He was talking to his fellow officers. "Get some body bags up here. We have found remains of what appear to be women."

In a short while, the officers came up with their load of gear and equipment.

Jeff stood silently by, watching the officers at work. One more officer crawled into the hole, and the others reached in with the equipment the guys inside asked for. For what seemed like a long time, they worked in silence. Then one of the men in the cave spoke up.

"Okay, we have at least four bodies here. We have photographed them, and have put their remains in separate bags. We will hand the bags out to the entrance, and you can carry them to the vehicles."

Jeff remained standing a short distance away, watching as the bags were handed out. They were just bags of remains, and not heavy, as the bodies had long since decayed and were really nothing more than skeletons with ragged pieces of disintegrating clothes. In his heart, Jeff wondered about the women who had lived in those bodies at one time. What fear, what agony, had they gone through in their last moments of life, as Oscar had tortured, abused and, no doubt, raped them, before killing them?

After several hours of work, the officers gathered up their gear, and got ready to head back to the SUVs.

"Let's get back to town," Pete said. "And thanks Jeff. You have been a tremendous help to us. I think we have the clues here to some of the missing people in our surrounding communities, not to mention that you saved Eileen from the same fate that befell these people."

When they got back to the station, Jeff saw a news-media vehicle parked in the visitor's parking lot. Suddenly, he was not feeling well. He felt suddenly weak.

"Jeff, are you all right?" Pete asked, noticing Jeff's face change as he pulled the SUV in behind the station, into the parking lot.

"Yeah, I think so. It has just been a difficult few days, that's all."

"Is there anything we can do for you?" Pete asked.

"No, I think I will just take an evening, sleep this thing off, and get this behind me."

"Good idea," Pete said. "If there is anything you need from us, let us know. Other than that we will be in contact with you. The keys to your truck are in the front office. Ask the girl at the desk. She will give them to you."

The SUVs parked in the back parking lot and the officers went to work, bringing in the evidence. Jeff was escorted in the back door and pointed toward the front desk. He stopped. "Uh, Officer Pete, would you mind getting the keys for me?" Jeff asked.

"Sure. I can do that," Pete responded, but then asked: "But why don't you want to get them yourself?"

"There is a news van out front, in the visitor's section of the parking lot, and I have no desire to talk to anyone," Jeff responded.

"I understand," Pete said. "I will get you the keys ... Oh, your truck is out back by the way. You should not have any trouble getting away from here. No one knows you are here."

Pete walked to the front desk, got the keys and brought them to Jeff.

In less than thirty minutes, Jeff was home again. He parked his truck, walked out to the pen where his dogs were. They were glad to see him.

"Hi, Max ... Brick. How you been?" The dogs responded cheerfully and excitedly. They didn't know that their master had not gone to work that day, but had instead shown police detectives around a crime scene.

In his mind, Jeff just wanted to forget the whole thing, except for one person. His mind kept wandering back to Eileen. He had rescued her, and saved her life. "I wonder what is getting into me," he thought. He called to his dogs. "Here boys," He motioned to them. "Come on, lets go in for the evening."

Jeff fed his dogs, and got himself a frozen pizza and put it in the toaster oven. This evening, as he was working his body mechanically, placing the logs in the stove and getting the fire going with small tinder and card board paper, his mind was on the events of the last few days. The little 'ding' sound from his toaster oven reminded him that his pizza was done. He got a can of pop from the fridge, and with a plate of hot pizza on the armrest of his chair, he sat by the fire, eating his supper.

He thought of Faye. It seemed he always thought of Faye. But tonight, he thought of her in a different way. He wondered what she would tell him, if he could talk to her. He was not sure. It was as if the painful and distressing last few days had opened a up reservoir inside him, which he had capped off for the last number years. For some reason, he felt himself caring again, but this time for a different person. He found he was caring for Eileen. He wondered where she was tonight and what was she doing?

Jeff finished his pizza and decided to turn in early. He needed to rest, and he hoped he would be able to go to work tomorrow. After putting a few more pieces of wood onto the fire, he closed the door on the stove, hoping that tomorrow would be a regular day again. He headed off to bed and, in a matter of minutes, he was out.

The alarm rang as usual again in the morning and he woke up more rested than he had in a while. He left for work, trying to find a way to turn his mind back to its normal pattern of life, the way it had been before this terrible incident.

The day at work was uneventful, except that his buddies at work wanted to know what had happened. They had heard on the news that Eileen Benson had been found by a local hunter, named Jeff Nolan. Jeff told his colleagues that he was not able to talk about it now, but that he would later. They respected his wishes.

Jeff had not listened to the radio yet, and was not eager too. As he was going for lunch, he saw the headline on the front page of a newspaper, resting on one of the lunch tables. ABDUCTED WOMAN FOUND AND RESCUED BY LOCAL HUNTER. His stomach did a quick somersault. "This is all over the place," Jeff thought. "How will I get out of this?"

The day went normally for Jeff, except that his mind was not at rest. When he got home, and walked into his house that evening, there was a message on his answering machine. He pushed the talk button. It was a female voice. "Hello, Jeff. It's Eileen Benson. I was wondering if I could meet with you. Would it work for you to call me? " She gave her number. Jeff stood there for a full five minutes. "So," he thought. "I didn't' just rescue her. I connected with her. Now she wants to talk with me."

Chapter 10

The next evening, after work, Jeff found himself on his way to the Café in Forest hill. It was a small, quiet place. Jeff didn't go there often, and not many people knew him. He had responded to Eileen's call and they had agreed to meet in there, the next evening at eight. Jeff wondered what she was up to. Had he missed something? Was she just calling him to thank him for having rescued her?

As Jeff pulled up to the curb outside the café, he suddenly found himself nervous again about talking to a woman even though he knew her.

Jeff walked in and paused for a second, letting his eyes get adjusted to the dim lighting. There she was, a slender figure in a booth by the wall. Jeff walked over to the table. She was reading a book, which she held in her left hand in front of her. In the other hand she held a cup taking a slow sip.

"Hi Eileen," Jeff spoke, awkwardly, not knowing what to say. "It's me, Jeff."

Eileen looked up from her book and set the cup down. She was a different person now. Under the doctor's treatment, the swelling in her face was as good as gone, and with some makeup the bruises were well concealed. She was wearing a red turtleneck sweater under her jacket, which complemented her fair complexion, hazel eyes, and brown hair.. She had a look of vibrant young beauty, which was intensified by the beautiful smile, with which she greeted Jeff.

"Oh, hi Jeff," she said pleasantly. "I'm so glad you came. Here, sit down. I want to talk with you. If that's okay with you, that is," she finished hastily.

Jeff accepted her invitation and sat down. A waitress walked over with a coffee pot and a cup. "Coffee?" she asked.

"Yes, please." Jeff responded. The waitress poured a cup and put some creamers beside it, before walking away.

Jeff put the cream in his coffee, added some sugar, and stirred. He raised his eyes, and found Eileen's looking straight into his."

"Jeff," she began. "I, uh ... I don't know where to begin, but something happened when you rescued me. I don't know what to say, or how to say it. But you are not like a normal man," She stopped talking as suddenly as she had begun. Then she started again. "I'm sorry. That just came out wrong. I'm not getting off on the right foot here. I would like to get to know you better, as a friend, I mean. Would that be okay with you? You have done so much for me, and there is no way I can ever thank you for your heroic efforts in saving me. Words don't do justice to your sacrificial acts of kindness toward me. After I was taken into the hospital, and the doctors questioned me, and treated me, the reality of all this hit. And then, yesterday, the police interviewed me and compared my story with yours. They told me I was the luckiest woman alive, to have been rescued by someone like you." She stopped suddenly again, just as she had begun, her eyes welling up with tears.

Jeff sat, slowly stirring his coffee. Presently, he looked up. He began to open his mouth, but then shut it again. He was not sure if he was ready to say what he felt like saying. Here was this woman, whose life he had rescued, who had told him that if she ever got back to civilization, she would never see or speak to another man again. And yet she had asked to meet him.

"Is something wrong?" She asked.

"No, I'm just thinking, I guess," Jeff responded.

"Thinking 'bout what?"

"About all that's happened in the last few days," he said softly.

"Jeff, I don't mean to be intrusive," Eileen began, "but after I was taken to the hospital to be checked out, my mind went back to you, and all that had happened. I could not shake you out of my mind. You are different. I think, for the first time in my life ever, that I have met a person who knows what they believe in, and why. I need to know what it is that you have that I don't. When I was in that hospital getting checked out, I had time to think, and I thought about you. I am not saying that I agree with your views on God, or prayer, even now. But I do know this. You have something that I have never seen, or heard before. I want to know what it is. Would it be possible for us to get together sometime, for a longer time, and talk?"

"What is it that you want to know about me, or about what I believe?" Jeff asked, wondering what it was about him that could possibly be of such interest to this young woman's mind.

"I'm not sure I know what I am asking for," Eileen responded. "Just to tell me about yourself, and why you did what you did."

"Eileen," Jeff began, "I'm just an average, ordinary man. That's all. I consider myself a very fortunate man, to have had a good upbringing, and having been given so much. I have had a fair share of tragedies happen to me, but I have much to be grateful for. This event, me rescuing you, was not really something that I would have considered myself capable of doing. When I was a young lad, my father told me that I had to decide early in life what I would do when it came to difficult choices. One of the things I learned, was that my father decided before hand how he was going to respond in times of testing. He didn't make the decision of what to do when the tests came to him. He decided his responses beforehand. That way he was always ready to do the right thing. But I have to be honest Eileen. I had never decided that, in a time like this, I would be actually ready to take the life of another human being, even to rescue an innocent victim. In a sense, I was not ready to kill Oscar. By the way, did you know that his name was not Bob?

Eileen nodded. "I know, the police informed me."

Jeff continued. "Back to answering your question - honestly I didn't know I would be prepared to do what I did. I just know I decided years ago, when I married my sweetheart Faye, that I would always do my best to protect her, no matter how high the cost was to me. I think what happened this last weekend was that my character was simply programmed to defend and protect innocent life more than I realized, and you were the recipient of that protection. I had no intention of hurting, or killing this kidnapper. What happened to him was his own doing."

"I get that part, Jeff." She said sweetly, and patiently. "It makes sense to me. But what I am wondering about is the underlying foundation here. What is it in you that makes you do this kind of thing? I mean, what made you save me the way you did at such risk? My experience with men has been different. I believe, just by observing you, that for you this is a way of life, is it not?" she looked at him, with questioning eyebrows.

"Yes, it's supposed to be," Jeff responded humbly. "That is part of my upbringing. I have been taught to always put the other person ahead of myself."

"Well, you sure went all out for me, when you found me."

Jeff looked up from taking a sip of his coffee. "Really I only did what any normal man should have done."

"True, but when you heard my scream, and saw the van, you could have turned around, walked away, pretended you had never seen or heard anything and simply gone home. No one would have ever heard from me again, and you would have been completely free."

"It may look that way to you," Jeff said, "but in reality, it is different. I would not have been able to do just nothing in that case. And I would not have been completely free, as you said. My conscience would not have permitted it. Even if I had done nothing, and had gone back to town, I would have had to call the police or something, to let them know. My conscience would have never let me rest until the matter was cleared up."

"You know Jeff, we could talk here for hours, but what I wanted tonight was to just see you, talk with you and ask you if I would be able to come over to your house for a visit? I mean ... I want to get to know you. I would really like that."

Jeff pondered for a moment before he spoke. His mind went back to Faye. He knew she would approve. He knew what he needed to do. "Okay, sure. I'm good with that. What do you have in mind?"

"I would like to come to your house, see where you live, and visit with you," she said. "I will be taking some time off from work, just to rest for a while and get my life back together again. How does Sunday sound? Perhaps we could visit then? Would that work?"

Jeff's mind whirled. 'Eileen wanted to come to his house, and have him spend time with her!' Her heart was going places where his was not ready to follow. But then, what did he have to lose? "Yeah, Sunday afternoon should be fine," Jeff responded. "Why don't you come over for two in the afternoon? I will be waiting". Then he looked closely at Eileen. "How are you holding up– I mean, this tragic event–how are you doing?"

Eileen looked at Jeff. "I'm not sure yet. All I know, for now, is that I have to be careful. My body is not quite back to normal, from last week. But I will be fine, I'm sure. Well," she said, "I don't want to stay long. I felt I just wanted to see you, and talk with you personally, and ask you if I could visit. I need someone to talk to, and I think you are the one. So, we will see each other on Sunday then." As she got up and began to walk toward the counter to pay, she turned back to look at him. "I will pay for the coffee." She laid some cash on the counter, turned and walked out the door.

Chapter 11

Jeff remained sitting at the table for a while. With Eileen gone, he had decided to sit for a bit longer, finish his coffee and then go home. Tomorrow would be another day.

As he sat sipping his coffee, the door of the café clanged open and three older gentlemen walked in. It was a bit too dim in the entrance for him to see who they were, but Jeff recognized their voices right away. It was Pastor Raymond, and church elders Ron Baxter and Carl Davis.

Jeff decided to remain sitting. He turned a little bit toward the wall, sitting so that he would not be recognized. He believed these men had probably come for a coffee, after having had one of their monthly church meetings. Hopefully, if he didn't look up from behind the collar of his winter coat, they would not recognize him, or suspect that he was there.

They sat down in the booth next to him. The wall separating his booth from theirs would keep him out of their view. "Thank God for dim-light coffee shops," Jeff thought to himself.

The waitress came and poured them their coffees.

"I'm telling you," Carl Davis began, as if continuing a conversation that had started some time before they had gotten to the coffee shop, "our brother, Jeff Nolan did a fine deed by rescuing that real estate agent, Miss Benson. Don't you think? Why, did you read in the paper what he did? As far as I'm concerned, I would be proud to be his father. I just don't get it, that some of our people from the church think he made a mistake, or worse, that he actually committed a sin."

Ron Baxter spoke up. "Listen, Carl. No matter how heroic you think Jeff Nolan was out there, rescuing this woman, he killed another man. It's just like I've been saying, It's against God's laws." It was clear that Ron was quite animated about this. He continued. "God will not let anyone go unpunished who sheds another man's blood. I'm surprised how many, including you, seem to think he did the right thing. I say that, as a church, we cannot let this incident go. Jeff killed another human being and we must do something about it. I just hope he is repentant and willing to make amends." He finished his sentence in a serious tone.

Carl interjected. "Make amends? Make amends for what, and to whom, Ron? You talk as if Jeff committed a sin."

"He did! He did commit a sin," Ron responded emphatically. "He killed another man, even though he said to the police that it was self-defence. He did shoot him, and I say he shot him in cold blood."

"Ron," Carl responded, tensely. "Think about this for a moment. Why, just Saturday morning my wife came home from the ladies' prayer meeting and said they had been praying for this poor real estate agent, praying that God would protect her and rescue her. They prayed that God would send someone to her aid her, and bring her back. When they had heard on the news that Miss Benson had been kidnapped, and her car had been found at the property, with blood inside the house ... they were afraid, not just for Miss Benson, but for their own safety. This abduction was any woman's worst nightmare come true. They were all afraid that she was gone for good, and so they prayed ... hoping that someone would come to her aid and help her. That was Saturday morning. And you know what; according to the paper it was Saturday morning that Jeff found this woman and risked his life to save her ... at the very time they had been praying for Miss Benson. I think that's pretty good, if you ask me. And not only that, did you read how they've found the remains of several other women as well, as the direct result of what Jeff Nolan did?"

Jeff sat silently on the other side of the booth wall, again thankful that the wall was so high that they could not see over. He was getting a good first-hand account of the feelings toward, or against him, out there.

Carl continued. "Ron, I think Jeff did the right thing but, from what I'm hearing from you, you believe that Jeff sinned in shooting the abductor, Oscar Ritchie. Can you explain that?"

"Well," Ron said, sounding as if he was sitting tall in the bench in his booth, "we know that vengeance belongs to God. He will avenge, he says. It is his to repay."

Carl responded calmly. "Who said anything about vengeance, Ron? And what is this you are talking about repaying? When Jeff found Miss Benson, he had no revenge on his mind, or any thoughts of killing him or anyone else. He wanted to set her free and get out of there. That is what he told the police in the report that they published in the newspaper. What should he have done? What are you calling vengeance here?"

"Well," Ron responded, again slowly, putting emphasis into his words. "He should have prayed, called the police, and left it at that. That is what he should have done. That is what I would have done." He had avoided answering Carl's question.

"Ron, it's obvious you have not read the write-up in the paper," Carl said. "According to the police interview, Jeff was out of cell phone range when this happened. There was no way of contacting police."

Ron was not deterred. "Jeff could have turned around, gone back to town, at least within cell phone reach, and called the police. At any rate, Jeff should not have taken matters into his own hands."

Carl was getting exasperated. "Ron you don't really believe that. You really don't, do you?" Carl asked, incredulously. "You say he should have prayed and called the police. Okay, granted. How do you know he didn't pray when he came on the crime scene and, even if he didn't, there were people who said they had prayed, had they not? And not only that, let me repeat, he was the only one available, and he was beyond cell phone signal. If Jeff had gone back to town, a few hours drive, called the police, and waited for them to come out that way, who knows what would have happened? They might never have found Miss Benson. Oscar might have taken off with her to who knows where? And if they finally did catch up to this killer, she might have been dead by then. No, Ron, it looks to me like, when it comes to compassion, or the letter of the law, what I am hearing from you right now is that you would rather choose the letter of the law and forget about mercy and compassion."

"I choose to do what God's laws demand. That's it," Ron responded confidently.

"Okay Ron, when you mentioned that Jeff should have called the police; let's take this a step further. How about the police then? Would you say that the police would have sinned by taking in Oscar Ritchie, and possibly ending up killing Oscar if he had put up a fight? Given that you say shedding man's blood is sin, does that mean for everyone, whoever does it, regardless of circumstances?"

"The law of the land is there to punish the evil doers, the bible says. That is not our job."

"Ron, you are avoiding my question," Carl persisted. "You say that shedding man's blood is sin. If you are consistent, than you have to say that killing Oscar was a sin no matter who did it, right?"

"Yes, killing Oscar was wrong. It was sin, no matter who did it." Ron responded, again with an air of confidence.

"Okay Ron, let's continue to follow your logic. If killing Oscar was sin, then for Jeff to call the police would have been a sin too – if the phone call had led to Oscar's death at the hands of the police. It would make Jeff a part of that event, since it would have been his phone call that brought the police out, enabling them to take Oscar down, and being forced to kill him as a last resort. That would make Jeff responsible for the death of Oscar that way, as well.

Ron started getting more animated. "I don't care what you say, Carl. I stick to what I understand the bible to say, and I will not be swayed by thinking like yours. Jesus taught us to turn the other cheek and not resist an evil person, and he didn't prescribe it only in certain circumstances," he finished tersely.

"I guess we are on different pages, on this matter," Carl said slowly. "I just have to say that I think Jeff did the right thing. I most certainly would be the first to affirm him for the actions he took. If Jeff had allowed this killer to take Miss Benson's life, without doing anything to attempt to rescue her, I would say that then he would have sinned. After all, there is also a verse in the bible that says anyone who knows the good he ought to do, and doesn't do it, sins. That is in the New Testament somewhere."

Ron spoke up. "Pastor Raymond, you have not said anything, yet. What do you think? I mean you have preached many sermons on love, on peace, and on non-resistance and non-violence. Jesus taught us to turn the other cheek, and not to resist an evil person, right? Don't you think that, as pacifists, we should not get ourselves involved in stuff like this, and instead leave it to the governing authorities?"

Pastor Raymond sighed deeply. He spoke up. "Ron, you are right in saying that I have preached many sermons on non-violence and peace. I will continue to preach those sermons. But I'm not sure that things are always the way they are perceived. And I do believe in turning the other cheek, and when the bible says we should not resist an evil person, I believe we should obey that too. But the interpretation is not understood the same by everyone. In fact, I don't believe that most people practice it the way Jesus intended it."

"What do you mean, Pastor?" Ron asked. "You're not saying that it is right to resist evil and take matters into our own hands, is it?"

Pastor Raymond paused, and then responded, thoughtfully. "My understanding of this passage has changed over the years. I used to believe it the way I just heard you explain yourself Ron, but I am not the same person I was many years ago, on this issue. Let me ask you something, Ron," Pastor Raymond spoke slowly. "I will give you an explanation, but first, tell me; how do you practice this teaching, this what you just mentioned - 'non-resistance' teaching?"

"I just live it out, just like it says. I don't resist an evil person." Ron said a bit too loudly. "I mean, I would not take matters into my own hands, if my safety or well-being was threatened. That is what we have the police for. God put them here to protect us. Our job is to trust God, and let the authorities he has appointed take care of the policing."

Pastor Raymond responded slowly, but deliberately. "You are right about a few things, Ron, but I question your statements about a few others. You say you 'just live it the way it is written'. Okay. But let me, if I may, peel back some layers and see what is inside at the core. I am not so sure about your stand on non-resistance Ron. You seem very confident, but I want to challenge you on that."

"How do you mean?" Ron asked, a bit uncomfortably.

"Let me tell you a story," Pastor Raymond began. "There were two guys who met in a community park; both had come there with their pickup trucks. These guys were just visiting, as friends often do. Unbeknownst to them, in the park on one of the walkways, among the bushes, a retired man was taking a leisurely afternoon walk, along with his little dog. He thought he was there alone, but then he heard voices. He stopped and listened as these two friends were talking. The two guys didn't realize that there was someone else there, nearby. The old man realized that these guys were beginning to argue. It had something to do with a deal about a truck trade. Both thought they were right, and the other was wrong. It got heated and angry between these two, as their voices rose into angry verbal assaults. At first, the retired gentleman thought he, just maybe, should walk into the open and let these guys see that he was there, but then thought he better just stay put and not let on that he was in the vicinity. and watch through the trees The verbal exchange grew louder and more vicious. They were calling each other names and threatening each other, with no one backing down. What happened next was tragic. One guy lost his temper, grabbed up a piece of heavy tree branch that was lying close by and, with full blunt force, cracked it on the other guy's neck, which broke instantly. The other guy dropped dead on the spot. Let me ask you, Ron, what should the old man have done who watched through the trees, and listened to all of this. Did he do the right thing by remaining hidden and not getting involved?"

Ron answered slowly, "Well, I can't say for sure. I don't know all the details."

"But Ron," Pastor Raymond persisted, "you said that we should not resist an evil person. For this man to have gotten involved, he would have had to do some resisting, would he not? What would you suggest that he should have done?"

"From the information that you have told me about this story, I say he did the right thing by not getting involved, as I see it. If he had tried to break up the argument he would have had to resist, yes. And he might just have increased the fight, or gotten hurt himself, him being an older retired man and all, you know. If he wanted to live by the teachings of our Lord, he would have walked away. Jesus did say that we should not resist an evil person," Ron finished, quite smugly.

"What about calling the police?" Pastor Raymond asked. "Should he have, at least, called the police when the guys started to fight?"

"I think so," Ron responded, hesitantly.

"But then the police would have had to do the dirty work of resisting and stopping the fight and enforcing order, the very thing that you say is sin, no matter who does it. And the resistance from the law would have been started by you, by making the call." Pastor Raymond finished.

Ron sat quietly, saying nothing as he looked at Pastor Raymond. He didn't like where this was going.

"Let me finish the story, Ron." Pastor Raymond went on. "The guys who were in the park with their trucks, were cousins. They had just purchased ice cream cones, from a stand down the street, and were talking together about their Tonka trucks. Toy pickups. The one had promised the other to make a trade, and now they were arguing about it. One of the guys was nine years old, and the other guy was ten. Does that additional information make a difference in how you would have responded, Ron?"

Ron was at a loss for words. "I ... I ... I guess so. He should have done something."

"But Ron," Pastor Raymond continued. "According to your own words, you said the elderly gentleman should have walked away. What changed?"

"I didn't know it was just school-age boys. That changes the story." Ron replied.

"No, Ron. The only thing that changed was your perception. You didn't know that it was two boys that had the fight. You thought it was two men. So now, don't you think stepping in between these two boys, and keeping them from hurting each other, would have been the right thing to do?"

"Yes, I agree," Ron said slowly.

"Would you say that stepping in between these two guys, and perhaps making sure that the one with the stick would not hurt the other one, would constitute 'resisting evil'?"

"I guess, so," Ron replied slowly, and a bit cautious.

"Well, then," Pastor Raymond spoke again, "tell me, at what age level should evil not be resisted anymore? How about if a fifteen and fourteen-year-old are fighting? Should someone resist that evil? How about a man beating his wife, should not someone resist that evil?

Ron remained silent.

Pastor Raymond just nodded slowly. "You see, Ron, sometimes we are too black and white. And it gets us into situations where, to follow the letter of the law, makes us militant pacifists ... militant pacifists who end up allowing innocent people to suffer by enabling perpetrators to continue their tyranny unrestrained and with no consequences. When we do that, we come out on the other side. What I mean is this; for the sake of following the letter of the law, we become fearful and unloving, hostile and militant people, who expect others to do the things for us that we say are wrong. In the end, we are not compassionate, and we are not caring. God becomes a cruel task master who demands obedience to the law, and love and justice are thrown out."

Pastor Raymond paused, and then continued on. "In the case of these two cousins, their lives were shattered. One was dead, and the other had this reality hanging over his head, that he had killed his best friend. And the old man in the park, who so easily could have resisted this youngster, didn't do a thing. Now, consider this, Ron. If one of your loved ones was in trouble, and I was in the vicinity, and I had the means and ability to come to their aid but, under the conviction of being a pacifist, I stood idly by while their life was ruined, or brutally ended, how would you look at me?"

Ron sat thinking, still remaining silent.

Pastor Raymond continued on again. "I see parents practising resistance all the time. And I am thankful they do. Parents who practice no resistance often raise children who are useless to themselves , to anyone else and eventually a problem to the community. Good parents use resistance in the home to keep their children in line, and from getting violent with each other. Police officers use it in law enforcement to protect communities. A man who beats his wife has to be resisted by other men. It would be evil to do nothing to restrain him. Not to resist an evil person is not what many pacifists make it out to be. I realize that many people in our tradition would say that there is no room for any resistance at all, but they forget that the moment they stand between a perpetrator and a victim, they are forming a resistance barrier. And often those very persons who stand up the strongest, for our pacifist views, are the most militant in enforcing them. They use the very means they condemn to enforce their position"

"Okay, Pastor, I think I see what you mean," Ron spoke up with a defensive note in his voice. "Then, explain to me what you mean when you preach, 'do not resist an evil person, and turn the other cheek. What does that mean?"

"I don't claim to have a full answer for you." Pastor Raymond responded. "There is much in scripture that I am still learning. If you had asked me this question thirty years ago when I was new in ministry, I would have had a lot of black and white answers for you. I don't anymore. I have more grace now than I did then. But here is what I can tell you ..." Pastor Raymond paused before continuing. "In the later years of my ministry, I have seen a fuller picture of how God operates." He spoke carefully. "A lot of people who claim to believe in non-resistance are the most resistant people one can find. It's about being in control of the lives of others. They will preach non-resistance on everyone else and, at the same time, they are most resistant of all. And they demand that everyone conform to their ways and ideas, and accept their opinions. People like this resist everyone who does not bow to their ideas and interpretations. They are anything but non-resistant. But at the same time, they have no problem on calling for the world to come and protect them if they are in trouble. So the police come to their aid ... and then they don't hesitate to call the policemen's actions sinful. It is simply not consistent, and it is wrong."

Pastor Raymond paused again for a moment and then continued. "And then on the other hand, I have come to know some very - to use your terminology Ron, some very non-resistant police officers. Maybe you find this hard to believe, but it is true. By non-resistant, I mean that they are the most open people, ready to listen, and give aid when and where they can. Many of them are the most gentle and firm people I know. They are very tolerant and will allow a person to hold to their own values and opinions. They will not resist a person's values or a person's beliefs, or even behaviour as long as they don't violate God's image—another human being. They will respond, with help, toward people who have nothing but ill will toward them. They will put themselves in harm's way to help those who want to do them harm. But they won't allow these same people to victimize and abuse other people. They are truly doing their jobs, as a service to the community and to God's glory. I know, I too call myself a pacifist. But I do stand against evil. The bible tells us not to resist an evil person, but then tells us to stand up for the cause of the innocent and the helpless. The bible tells of many cases were God's people confronted and challenged evil. In that sense, they were very resistant. The devil comes in many different means, ways, shapes and forms. Sometimes resisting the devil may mean standing up against some thing that is going on, but should not be going on. I know that the bible says we should not kill. With the command to not kill comes the self-understood principle that we need to protect life. I believe with the command to not kill sometimes comes the responsibility to do what we can to stop others from killing as well. Unfortunately, some people only understand the language of force. And I am not talking about violence. I think there is a difference between force and violence.

"What do you mean?" Ron questioned.

Pastor Raymond continued. "The difference between violence and force is this; a mother sees her three-year-old son has a stick and is about to beat his little two-year-old brother. She, forcefully, pulls her three-year-old away from his little sibling, before the stick lands on the little guy's head. Was she violent? No, she was not. Did she use force? Yes. She did the right thing. Was she resistant? Yes. And I would say that age is no barrier. If you see an adult do something that will hurt or harm another person, we are just as responsible, to do what we can to stop a violent action from happening. Of course, there are times when we are powerless to do anything. A ten-year-old seeing two men beat each other would not get involved. That is self evident. And every person knows, in their innermost being, if they have done what they could do remedy a bad situation."

Carl, who had, for a long time, not spoken a word, now spoke up. "Thanks, Pastor Raymond, I thought you had these views, but I was not sure. I agree with you, that there is a lot that we don't understand. And in this case, the case with Jeff, my suggestion is that we make it as comfortable and gentle for him as possible. I can just imagine the pain he must have been through, in being forced to make such a difficult decision. At this time, to come down on him with a demand for repentance and amends would not show love or compassion. If anything, it would come to him as a Pharisaical practice of the law. And I would not want to be part of something like that."

"I have been meaning to get a hold of him," Pastor Raymond spoke again. "But I have not gotten to it yet, for a few reasons. Jeff has not been in church on a steady basis for some time, and only recently has been coming more steady again. I thought I would see if he shows up for church this weekend, and try to connect with him, to see if we can have coffee. I have good hopes for him. He is a strong man. If we, as brothers, rally around him and welcome him, we will do him a great service. Now is not the time to debate with him on the right and wrong of taking a human life. I'm confident that he did what he believed honoured God in that moment, as much as we regret how things turned out. It was not Jeff who created the circumstances. Evil created the circumstances, and evil was defeated. For that, I am thankful. Anyway men, I think it's time to go home."

The three men got up, paid for their coffee and walked out. Jeff waited till they were gone, and then walked out of the café to his truck and drove home. He knew in his heart that he had some good friends at the church, and was not worried anymore about how his church community would take what had happened.

Sunday morning was crisp and clear and Jeff was wide awake early. He fed his dogs and got into his Sunday best to go to church. The night in the café in Forest hill had been good for him. Not one of the three men who had been in the café knew that he had heard the whole conversation. He was glad to know that most of the people were for him, and not against him. It felt good to be respected for having done a difficult, but good, thing.

Somehow, this morning, thinking about Faye as he got out of his bed, he realized that he was still missing her, but not in the same way as before. It was as if the ice was melting. There seemed to be a breeze in his soul. Outside, in the physical world, it was cold, and winter was coming fast, but it seemed that in his heart spring was finally coming. Who knew what time would bring?

The church service that morning was the same as usual. Pastor Raymond spoke on love and the bible, and pointed out that, no matter who we claim to be, what good we claim to do, unless we do it in love, we are nothing.

Jeff's mind wandered over to Elder Ron Baxter. "I wonder if he is thinking about how I killed Oscar," Jeff wondered. "Perhaps he's wondering how the idea of love fits into all of this." Jeff tried to concentrate on Pastor Raymond's preaching, but noticed his mind wandering again to Ron Baxter, and the conversation he had overheard earlier in the week.

Pastor Raymond next comments brought Jeff back to reality. "Sometimes, to show love is the most difficult thing," he was saying. "If you truly love, there may be times when you will show that love by taking a stand for the right thing, in a way that may cost you everything you have. And there are times in life when you cannot take a stand against wrongness by walking away from it. Sometimes you have to confront it. If love believes all things, endures all things, that may mean you will be faced with the decision to confront evil—by taking a position where how things will turn out is an uncertainty. As human beings, we are responsible for the well-being of everyone in our homes, our comunities and our society. Sometimes, doing the loving thing means getting in the way of the wrong and giving another person our protection.

Jeff was all ears now. "I know he is thinking about my situation," Jeff thought. "I know this much; he is not against me, that I know for sure. Maybe he is doing this to give a lesson to the people, so they are not hard on me for what I did."

After the service, on the way out, Jeff walked by Pastor Raymond as he shook the hands of the parishioners walking out the door. "Good to see you Jeff," Raymond said. "Let's have coffee some time. Would that work for you?"

"Yeah, sure," Jeff responded. "When would you like?"

"How about Wednesday evening? Meet me at the café in Forest Hill at seven?"

"Okay, I will be there."

Jeff drove home and got something to eat, and then tidied up his house. Eileen would be coming over in less than two hours. Somehow, her coming over made him feel different, as if he was glad to see her. He checked his thoughts. "I don't really even know her. Her world views are drastically different than mine. I better get ahold of myself, or I will do something I may regret later," he told himself.

Chapter 12

Eileen was deep in thought as she got herself ready to drive over to Jeff's place. In her mind, she was wondering why she was doing this. She didn't even know the man. At the same time, she had a desire to just meet with him again and get to know him.

As she flipped through her wardrobe, she wondered what would be good to wear on this occasion, at this time of year. She realized that she was fairly self-conscious of her looks. She picked out a dark brown turtleneck sweater, and pants to match. She figured it might be cold and this would protect her from the elements. Next, she went before the mirror to make sure her hair was in place, and put on some makeup.

Ruby Miller, her co-tenant in the apartment, walked by the bathroom and saw Eileen putting on makeup. She stood for a moment, watching her. "Eileen, it looks like you are going out to see someone special. Are you?"

"Well, yes sort of," Eileen responded, as she was putting on the finishing touches to her face.

"Anyone I might know?"

"If you have read the papers, you have heard about him," Eileen responded.

"Oh, are you talking about the guy who rescued you?" Ruby asked.

"Yes, that's him." Eileen responded, hoping that Ruby would not be too nosey. The last week had not been easy for her. There were too many questions raging through her mind. She still could not shake the thought that, for all intents and purposes, she should be dead. But now she was alive and well. Her pain was pretty much gone, and so were the bruises.

Even though she had declared to herself, during that ordeal out in the wilderness, that she would never have any contact in any way with another man ever, and had said as much to Jeff after he rescued her, today was different.

"Well, I wish you a good time, Eileen," Ruby said, interrupting her train of thought.

"What did you say?" Eileen caught herself in her train of thought.

"I just said that I wish you a good time," she repeated.

"Oh, thanks. Thank you, I will see you later this evening," Eileen said.

Eileen took her purse, walked out of the apartment and got into her Ford Focus. She drove out to Jeff's place. While driving the distance to his place, she wondered what kind of man she would meet. Something was different today. She would have never in her wildest imagination dreamed that she would one day again have a desire to see and talk to a man, like she now wanted to with Jeff. There was something about him that drew her. She was determined to find out what it was.

The place where Jeff lived was just as he had described to her in the coffee shop. It was a simple place. It was obvious that there was not a high-class person living here.

She slowly drove up the driveway. Jeff's truck was parked close to his shop. Her mind wandered back to the place where Jeff had found her and how he had rescued her. She wanted to get to know this man.

She got out of her car, walked up to the door, and knocked. Out here in the country, it was a bit breezy. She drew her winter coat close over her sweater to keep warm. She heard a bark inside the house and thought; "Oh no ... dogs." She had forgotten about those dogs. She didn't like dogs. Then she heard a muffled voice in the house and then silence.

The next moment, she heard the door knob turn, and the door opened. There was Jeff. He was wearing a pair of jeans, a sweater, and was holding a cup of coffee in his hand.

"Hi, Eileen, it's good to see you!" he exclaimed. "Come in." Jeff stepped aside and motioned with his free hand.

Eileen stepped into the house, and her eyes did a brief scan. "What am I doing?" she thought. "Here I am again, with another strange man in another strange house." She focused her thoughts. She had come here for a purpose and she would find out what it was about this man that drew her to him. He had accepted her request to see him, and she would not back out now. He had not once given her any reason not to trust him.

"Here, let me get your coat, while you sit down and make yourself comfortable," Jeff said, motioning to his living room set. "Can I get you something to drink, a coffee maybe?"

"Yes, thank you."

Jeff put her coat in the closet, walked over to the kitchen counter and got a cup from the cupboard.

"How do you take your coffee?"

"I take it just black, thank you."

Jeff poured a cup of steaming coffee from the pot on the coffee maker's element. "Here," he said, as he handed her the cup.

"Thanks."

She took a sip of her coffee, while Jeff took his cup off the counter, and walked over to the easy chair beside the love seat, where Eileen had sat down. Her eyes took in the small house, its furnishings, and décor. She noticed, on the book shelf, a picture frame of a beautiful woman, and realized that it must be Jeff's special someone. She decided not to ask about that now. That time would come later. She sipped her coffee again. No one spoke.

Jeff was wondering about all the things that had prompted Eileen to want to come over and pay him a visit. He remembered the conversation in the coffee shop, earlier that week, and he wanted to give her time to come out with her questions. Also, he had some deep questions of his own. He took another sip from his coffee, and spoke up. "Eileen, I don't know what your plans are for this afternoon. Did you have something in particular in mind? If not, I was wondering if we could go for a walk. There is a narrow lane-way behind my place where I usually go for walks. It runs by a farm behind my property here. That is, if it's not too chilly for you."

"Oh, Okay, that sounds good," Eileen responded. She was hoping to find the courage to come out and ask Jeff the questions that were simmering in her mind, but now didn't seem like the best time to do that.

"Okay, we will go in a few minutes." He changed the subject. "By the way, how are things going for you?" Jeff sipped his coffee again. "Are you back to work yet?"

"I'm starting this week. But I won't be doing any showings." Eileen responded. She gave Jeff a brief description of what her work would be now. She would be in the office, handling phone calls for the next several months. She needed time to heal, but she also needed the work to pay her bills.

"I understand," Jeff replied. "I think you are making a good decision to stay in the office for now. Here, why don't we get started on our walk?" Jeff remarked, getting up and putting his cup in the sink.

The dogs were in the other room, and heard their master, Jeff, talk about walking, and began whining. "Max, Brick, this walk is not for you, be quiet." The dogs quieted down. "Don't mind the dogs Eileen, they won't bother you."

Jeff got Eileen's coat out of the closet and handed it to her, and then got out his own winter jacket, put it on, and stepped outside.

"Let's go this way," Jeff motioned toward the back of his property, to the lane-way running alongside the field. "It's a really nice place to walk. There's no traffic, except once in a while in the summer when the farmer uses that lane to get to his property."

"I'm with you Jeff. You lead the way."

This Sunday afternoon, there was a breeze, but only a light one. Jeff enjoyed walking and he felt better. They walked in silence for a few minutes. It seemed that neither knew what to say, or wanted to say anything.

Eileen rehearsed in her mind the things that she had gone over, mentally, during the last few days. She wanted to know what Jeff had that she didn't. She decided she was going to ask.

"Jeff," Eileen began, "I don't know how to say this, or how to start. I'm sure you may have wondered why I initiated a visit with you, even though I mentioned some things in the coffee shop last week. I just need to talk to you, and see where things are at." She paused for a moment, and then began. "Before I met you, or I should rather say, before you met me, I was busy with real estate, and my life was good and satisfying—at least,

I thought it was. But then, when I was kidnapped, I thought for sure my life was over. Then, out of nowhere, you came along and rescued me. It was what happened in those hours, while you were there with me, trying to find a way out of the mess we both were in, that I realized that what I had was not all there was. I was afraid I was going to die. I saw you had fear too, but you had something stronger than fear. You had courage. You have strength that I just don't know about ... I mean, spiritual strength, if that is what you call it. I guess what I'm saying is that I am interested in knowing about what it is that makes you ... you."

They were walking slowly, side by side. Jeff pondered her question. After a lengthy quiet time, Eileen looked up at him, with her eyes, as if wondering if Jeff had heard her. Jeff noticed her questioning eyebrows and hastened to respond.

"Uh, yes Eileen, I hear you. You are asking a very deep question. And I'm not sure I have an answer for you, but let me try." Jeff again paused. "Suppose that..." he paused again.

"Yes?" she asked, waiting for him to continue.

"Suppose, Eileen," Jeff began, "that your body was not your body. Let's say you were just given occupancy of it ... rental possession of it, for just a while. And suppose you were given a detailed set of instructions on how to take care of that body while you were living in it. And suppose that you knew the owner of that body was, one day, going to come back and take that body, in which you now live, back. Now, also suppose that the owner of that body promised to give you an even better body, after he takes this one back. What impact would that make on how you would treat that body?"

"I'm not sure I'm following," Eileen responded, looking a bit puzzled. "What does that have to do with strength?"

"It's kind of like this, Eileen. The things we do make a difference depending on what kind of view we have of life, of ourselves, of the future, and of other people. It all interacts. As human beings we are not alone. Our actions influence and impact each other, in more ways than we can imagine. You mentioned that you saw strength in me. That may be what you saw, but the foundation of what you saw may not be clear to you. It is like seeing an iceberg, where what you see is only ten percent of the actual thing. The rest is invisible, hidden beneath the water."

"I think I get some of it, but I'm still not sure I understand. Please, tell me more," Eileen said, a bit puzzled.

"Let me try this, Eileen," Jeff said, "When I heard you scream, and I walked over and saw the blue van, I knew at that time what was required of me. I was under the strongest compulsion to go and rescue whoever it was that was inside that van. But that compulsion was not a normal compulsion. It came from deep inside me. Actually, it didn't come so much from me, as from someone who controls me, or rather, from whom I take instructions. One who owns, influences, and controls me. But also, inside of me, there was a lot of fear. I don't own this body in which I live. My only desire at that time was to use this body to come to the aid of another person who was in trouble. And so, when I found you, I was not thinking so much of myself, personally, as I was about the person needing my help. This body is just a rental to me. I have to give it back one day. I am free however, to make the decisions as to what I will do with this body, and what I will use it for. My goal is to live in this body, this rental property, as long as I am given opportunity, and after that, I will let it go, and I will get a new one. I think it is safe to say that my strength comes from an awareness that I am not alone, and that I am being observed at all times. And, the one who is watching me, gives me what I need when I need it. "

"Where do you get this stuff, Jeff?" Eileen asked, looking even more puzzled now.

"What stuff?" Jeff asked.

"This stuff about ... about ... you know, what you just said."

Jeff chuckled. "I need to start from the beginning Eileen. How much time do you have?"

"I got all afternoon, if that is what it takes."

"Okay, then let me begin from the beginning," Jeff said. "I have always believed, from the teachings of my parents, from the teachings of my Sunday school teachers, from the teachings of the bible, and from my elders in the church, that life is created by God. As human beings, we are all made in God's image. He has given us life, as we know it. And he has given it to us for a brief time, to enjoy it and to live for God's glory and the benefit of each other. So, we have this thing in us called life. But we don't own it. God is the giver and the taker of life, and life itself is sacred. It is for that reason that we must respect life. Life is that which has the highest value on earth. Nothing can substitute for it. There is simply no price you can put on life. The value of life is constant, throughout time and space. The value of life is not dependant on intelligence, or stage of development, or anything like that." At this point Eileen interrupted him.

"But Jeff, you talk about life as a sacred thing, and yet you are a hunter, killing animals. At least you were on a deer hunting trip when you found me. Is that not a contradiction? How do you reconcile that?"

For a moment Jeff was silent, and then responded. "When God created this world he put humans as the highest order of creation, to take care of this world for his glory. There is a difference between human life and the life of an animal. I believe as part of God's creation, killing and eating meat is not wrong. Killing an animal for food, or killing animals that are pests is not the same thing as killing people. I was hunting deer for the purpose of food, and to get away from work for a while. I would never kill an animal inhumanely for the desire to see pain and suffering." Jeff was not sure if he was doing a good job of explaining his views to Eileen. It seemed this would take time.

"Jeff, you have a very different view of life from what I have believed. In fact, I have to say I have never heard of views like yours until today. I will need time to think. Sorry for interrupting."

Jeff gathered his thoughts from where he had left off. "As I was saying earlier, when it comes to one's personal value of life, it doesn't matter what religion people come from, or what they believe or don't believe. People usually value their own lives. Most people will do anything it seems they need to do to live. The methods and means of expressing that desire to live, of course, differ vastly. People approach the focus of life differently. Sad to say, some people are predatory toward people. They will do what they can to live, but at the expense of other people. People like that live very empty and hollow lives. People like that will demand, from the lives of others, what they believe will benefit their own life. That is a self-focus. But not all people are like that. I thank God that there are people who look beyond themselves, and try to find ways in which to invest their lives into the lives of others and, in that way, expand their own lives. That is community. But let me focus on the selfish part for a moment." Here, Jeff paused for a moment and then continued.

"Take, for instance, Oscar Ritchie. My mind is on him a lot. I know it was through my hand that he died. And I didn't end his life because I thought his life had less value somehow. His life had the same value to me as does anyone else's life. Oscar had degraded himself to the point where he was totally bent on destroying life in whatever way his selfish desires craved, and that had to be stopped. I know that people could argue that I killed him, which is true. But it also needs to be pointed out that I rescued one person, and who knows how many more. Oscar was a man who may have had a rough start, perhaps, but he made a decision that he was going to get as much out of life as possible, at the expense of other people. It was not that he didn't want life. He wanted life. Oscar just wanted, not only his life, but the lives of those around him too. And there was something different about him. His desire for life was not a desire in the way he was created. Oscar was a defaced image of his creator. He allowed evil to control him, and it became his destruction. By allowing himself to become controlled by evil, he had a craving for destruction. He was not normal, and he let his evil control him, to the point that he resorted to kidnapping, torture, and killing to get what he wanted. That is an extreme expression of evil. I am thankful that not all people are like that."

Jeff continued as they walked. "As I said earlier, there are those people who think of the needs of others before their own. They will feel the pain of the other person, and they respond with compassion, mercy and love. These are people who are owned and possessed by a higher power. It is not that they are owned against their will. They surrender to a power that they want to submit to. But, as they submit to this higher power, and this power takes over, they are truly in tune with the one who made them, and who guides and controls them. It is like a sweet surrender, to a love and grace that has to be experienced to be understood. When I talk of this 'higher power,' I mean God himself."

"What is it that makes people like that? I mean good, self-sacrificing and ... like you described?" Eileen asked.

Jeff looked at Eileen for a moment. "I'm not sure how best to explain it to you, but here is what I believe. It comes down to a relationship with a person. I am a believer in God, as you already know. But it is more than that. I believe that God is the one who gives life, and he gives it through his son, Jesus Christ."

"Jeff," Eileen looked up at him, "I struggle with that. I have heard of Jesus, but never gave him a moment's thought. I have to be honest, and tell you that I am not where you are, and again, I don't know if I ever will be. Your faith may work for you. In fact, I have seen that it does. But I have to process this. I know I believed that the life I had before I met you was good. But I have seen something in you which I find very attractive, and at the same time very scary. I am very scared of giving up control of my life."

Jeff listened as Eileen talked. After she was quiet for a bit, Jeff responded. "I think you need to look from a different perspective, Eileen. How much control did you have when you were abducted?"

"Well," she said, "I was not in control. That freak that kidnapped me was in complete control."

Jeff asked, "What if I told you that no matter what circumstance you face, you can be in control of yourself at all times, no matter what you are going through."

"That sounds exciting, but unbelievable," Eileen responded.

"Well, it's true. You can have complete and total control, by giving up control. It is like an eagle stretching out its wings, and surrendering its body to the air currents as it floats in the wind."

Eileen looked a bit puzzled again, deep in thought.

Jeff continued. "Another way to look at this is to look at yourself as a tool in the master's hand. He is the one who is using his tools to do his work. The tools don't make the decisions as to exactly how they are going to be used. I know the analogy is not perfect, but go along with me for a bit on this one. We, as human beings, know almost nothing about life, the origin of life, or the future of life. We didn't decide to be born here, or anywhere for that matter. We were simply put here by someone who didn't ask us. That someone put us into the care of people we didn't know, or ask to be put with. That someone also has our life in his hands at all times. We are not independent or self-sufficient. Every one who is a human being is dependant on God's continuing power to sustain their life. If God pulls back his hand, we die."

Eileen listened thoughtfully. This was new to her. She was trying to absorb what Jeff was telling her, but she was not satisfied. "Okay," she said. "I'm not sure if I understand it all, but it somewhat makes sense. What puzzles me though, is ... why all this talk of living a 'good life', if we are so helpless, and can't do anything about our circumstances? I mean, a person is born into whatever situation they are born into, right? They can't do anything about it."

"It's not about living a good life, Eileen," Jeff responded. "Sure, we are supposed to live a good life, but that is not the point. When we are living as tenants in God's house, we honour and respect his property because we respond in love to what we have been given. We are his, for him to use for his glory in whatever way he sees fit. Sure, we want to live a good life, and for the most part we may succeed. But that is not because we have to. It's because we get to. There is a difference you know. We rise to a higher level of living. We become free."

"I think I am beginning to see," Eileen responded. "Kind of like two lovers, right?" she asked, as she looked up at Jeff, but then immediately blushed a bit, realizing how Jeff could take this.

Jeff looked down at her with his keen eyes, and answered her with a smile. "Yes, you got it. Just like two lovers. They do good things for each other, not because they have to, but because they can and because they want to."

"So then, when you talk about living a good life, and about having a relationship with God, it is about a relationship that is just as real between the person and God as it is between two people?" Eileen asked.

"That is what I mean, yes." Jeff responded. "However," he added, "that is something you have to come to on your own. That is not something any human being can do for you. You have to decide in your own soul if that is something that you want. Just like no person can make you like someone, or love someone, this is something that has to come out of your own heart."

"It is there for me too, if I want it?" Eileen asked.

"Yes, it's for everyone, you included."

"I will think about this."

They had turned around and were getting close to Jeff's place again. Jeff commented about the cool weather and asked if Eileen wanted to come in and warm up before she left.

"No, I don't think so. I have had a very good time, Jeff. You have helped me see life with a different set of lenses this afternoon. I feel you have something that I want. Let me think about it for some time. Would it be okay if I call you and come over again some time?"

"Sure," Jeff replied, "Whenever you feel like it. And, if you are interested, there are other people who have a lot more insight and experience in this life than I do. You might be interested in meeting some of them sometime, but just remember, Jesus is not something you add to your schedule like another 'to do' thing. If a person wants a relationship with him, it is not one of many things in that person's life. Jesus becomes the

Savour, the Lord, and the Master ... the friend, the sustaining power, and the guide over all of life."

"I will think about what you said," Eileen responded. "How would I best get to know some of the people you think I should meet?"

"Well, you could come to church on some Sunday morning, if that would interest you. I'm sure you would be welcome."

"I will think about it." With that, Eileen was at the door of her small car and getting in. "Thanks again Jeff, I had a very good time. See you later."

"Have a good evening," Jeff heard himself saying, as the motor started, and he stepped away from the little car.

In a minute, she was out of the drive way and down the road. Jeff stood there for a few minutes, pondering what had just happened. He felt a warm feeling in his heart that had not been there for a long time. He felt that his life-ship was not so stuck in the ice anymore. The dark cold night in his soul was lifting. It was beginning to dawn, and the ice was melting. It felt as if his ship was gently moving.

Chapter 13

Wednesday evening, Jeff arrived at the Café on time. He was looking forward to his Pastor's visit. As Jeff walked into the coffee shop, he saw Pastor Raymond already sitting in the booth—the very same booth he had been in the last time, when he'd heard the discussion with Ron and Carl.

Jeff walked over to Pastor Raymond. "Good evening Pastor," Jeff greeted him.

"Oh, good evening. I didn't see you walk in. Here, have a seat. How are things, Jeff?"

"Alright, I guess. It has been hard the last while, but I think I'm holding my own."

The waitress came with a cup, a pot of coffee and creamers. "Do you need a menu?" she asked.

"No, coffee is fine." Jeff replied.

She poured him a cup of coffee, put a few creamers down on the table and walked away.

"Jeff, I wanted to have coffee with you to simply see how things are going for you. If you are interested in talking about your recent experience, or anything else for that matter, I am here to listen. If you would rather not talk now, that is fine too. I'm here as your friend, to listen to you, and be here for you. From the police reports in the paper, I know what happened. I'm here to tell you that I am proud of you, and have no qualms about how you handled the situation you faced."

Jeff sipped his coffee for a moment, and then looked up. "I just want to say thank you for inviting me. It's special. I don't mind talking about what happened. What would you be interested in knowing?"

"It doesn't matter to me, Jeff. Whatever it is that is on your heart. But, since you asked, I am interested in how what happened to you, and this woman that you rescued, has affected you in recent days? I know that it is all very new still, and you may still be sorting out your thoughts."

"I don't really know what to say, except that I would have never believed I would face what I faced that Saturday morning on my hunting trip. I definitely was not hunting for what I got, that's for sure. It was the most frightening ordeal I have ever faced. I was scared but, at the same time, sensed a responsibility to this strange woman that I have never felt before. I knew that I might not survive, but I could not just let it go. I know I made the right move in trying to rescue this woman but, after I got kidnapped too, I realized that, unless a miracle happened, I would be killed first, and the woman next, and then who knew how many more after that. I had to do something." Jeff paused. Both of them sat for a moment sipping their coffee.

"Pastor," Jeff began again. "I have been thinking about this whole thing. I realize that there are people who no doubt disagree with me on what happened, I mean how I handled this situation. It remains to be seen what the law will do with me. I am trusting that I will get off free, for having done what I did. But in a way, deep inside me, there is pain because of how it ended for Oscar. And then there is his dad. I hear he is mean, old and cranky. He lost his only son. And there is nothing I can do about this now. But at the same time I feel very good for having rescued Eileen. Tell me pastor, how are the people in the community in general, and especially the church people, responding to this? I'm curious."

In his heart, Jeff already knew Pastor Raymond's mind on this matter, but he didn't tell him that.

"Well, Jeff, I can tell you this much. You won't have anything to worry about, from where I stand. I am not going to judge your actions. There are people who would say that what you did was wrong and, according to the letter of the law, they would be right. If the letter of the law was applied at face value, then to kill someone would be a sin, regardless of how it happened, because the bible does say 'do not kill.' But if the letter of the law were applied equally across the board, then none of us would ever stand a chance at life. Sometimes, if we are faithful, we get into a situation out of which there is no black and white way out. No matter how you handle it, there will be people who will think you failed." He quickly added, "That however is not to say that, in this instance, you failed."

Then he continued more slowly. "If someone would want to call your actions wrong, I would say that to do nothing would have been more wrong than to do what you did. From what I have been hearing, the majority of people are just grateful that you did what you did, and the way you did it. You went out on a limb, risking your own life for the benefit of another. Most people think you are a true gentleman. I don't think you have anything to worry about as far as the congregation is concerned. There have been a few voices telling me we need to make this a congregational matter. But I will do what I can to prevent that. There are a few people who are quite militant in trying to force me to do something about this, but, in their militant attempts at imposing their pacifist interpretations, they are saying more about themselves than anything else. My advice to you at this point is not to worry. I would say that, in this case, my personal opinion is that I think God is pleased with you, and you should feel at peace over the course of actions that you took. You have my blessing Jeff. There are times when, through no fault of our own, we are placed into circumstance, in which any course of action we take is going to be labelled as wrong by one party or another. That simply cannot be avoided. There are situations in life where there is no straight, pain free way out. No matter what you do, or don't do, you'll come out looking like you've done the wrong thing, to someone. I realize that there are people who would say that there is always a right way out but, of course, those people usually mean 'their' right way out. I just wish you God's peace and blessings."

"Thanks Pastor," Jeff replied. "There is another thing on my mind."

"What is that, if I may ask?" Pastor Raymond probed.

"You know that I have been a widower, for four years now. You and Betty walked with me through my darkest days, as I grieved and felt I could not go on without Faye in my life."

Pastor Raymond slowly nodded as Jeff spoke.

"I have been thinking. Is it possible to forget, and move on? I mean, what if someone else came along? What should I do?"

Pastor Raymond looked at Jeff for a moment. "Jeff, I think that the someone with the same power and strength that sustained you in the past, in your time of grief and loss over Faye, and also as you rescued this woman ... that same someone will be there to guide you when the time comes. It is possible for a man to have the courage and boldness of a lion in the face of danger but, in the presence of female love, become insecure and small. The power of a woman over a man is simply a mystery which, I believe, no one has really solved to this day, and I don't think anyone ever will. If God should bring another woman into your life, my advice to you would be to go slow, and wait for his timing. Sometimes, men find themselves in a very weak and vulnerable position, especially in the area of being attracted to a woman. But that is not to say that you should not love another woman. I'm simply saying to take it easy, and carefully work it through, before you allow your heart to be drawn in by a woman."

Pastor Raymond continued. "I know what Faye meant to you. But you need to think what she would want for you, if you could talk to her today. One thing she would not want for you, would be to be in depression and fear. She would want you to love life and enjoy the blessings God brings your way. Don't you think I am right about this?"

"Yes, I know you are." Jeff responded. "I think I need to just start admitting that my heart yearns for companionship, and when I was with Eileen, on that trip home, it was scary for me to realize that I was in the presence of a woman who depended on me, whose life was in my hands, and whose life I could help make whole, or destroy."

Jeff continued. "At this time, I don't know what I am feeling. But I know this. I want to open myself up again to love, to live and to enjoy life. This last week has been an eye opener for me in a lot of ways. It seems to me that there is a warm breeze beginning to blow where before there was nothing but a cold dark night."

"Well, Jeff, I'm glad to hear that. It's getting a bit late now. It has been a good evening. I will get the coffee," Pastor Raymond remarked.

"Thanks Pastor" Jeff replied.

The way home was a good drive for Jeff. It felt like he had been fed in his heart and soul. Pastor Raymond's advice was like a healing touch to his heart.

He parked his truck by his shop, plugged in the block heater, and walked into the house. In a matter of minutes, he was in bed and asleep.

Chapter 14

A few weeks later, one evening after Jeff got home from work, the phone rang. It was Eileen. "Hi Jeff," she began. "Are you busy tonight? If not, I was wondering if we could meet again. Would you be up for it? I would just like to talk."

Jeff paused for some time. He was not sure but, at the same time, felt quite at peace and not threatened by it. "Okay, sure. What did you have in mind?"

"I was thinking of perhaps meeting in town. We could have dinner together."

Jeff decided to go for it. They agreed on a place and time. An hour later, Jeff was in town at the diner Eileen had suggested. She was already inside, sitting at a table and looking at a menu when he walked in. He walked over to her table and sat down. She had taken a menu for him as well.

A waitress came with coffee and said she would be back shortly to take their orders.

"Jeff," Eileen began. "I have been thinking some more, since I was at your place."

Jeff listened without making any comment. Eileen continued. "I have been thinking about you, mostly. And then when I was in your house I didn't say anything, but I saw a picture of a woman on the book shelf. Who was she?"

Inwardly, Jeff's thoughts went quickly back to the visit Eileen had paid him. He was not sure if he was ready to share with Eileen, about Faye, and what she had meant to him. But then again, why not? "The picture that you saw on the shelf was a picture of my wife, Faye. But that picture is quite old, now. It was taken a few years before her death."

"I'm sorry, what happened?"

"I don't know really. The doctors said she had contracted a serious flu virus. It took her life."

The waitress came with the food and set the plates in front of them. Jeff looked at Eileen and offered to give thanks for the food. Eileen just nodded and followed his lead. Jeff gave a short prayer of thanks to God, for his blessings and the time he was able to spend with Eileen.

After eating for a few moments in silence, Eileen spoke up. "Jeff, if you don't mind my asking, I would like to know about you and your life, and and tell me some more how you came to be where you are today."

Jeff wondered what Eileen had meant on the phone when she'd said she would like to talk. Had she meant that she would like him to talk and she would just listen to him? If she wanted to talk, why was she asking him questions? He decided now was not the time to see how strong their fragile relationship was. He was going to be open with her.

Jeff shared with Eileen his early years as a young boy on the farm with his parents, and how he had enjoyed hunting with his father and brothers. He had lived a simple but good life. Then later, when he had fallen in love with Faye, he and Faye had believed they were going to enjoy life together in married bliss. He told her about discovering that Faye couldn't have children, and trying that much harder to be a good husband to her. And he told her that when Faye had died, he had felt at his lowest point in life.

When Jeff mentioned that they had not been able to have children, Eileen lowered her eyes and seemed to lose some interest. Jeff noticed it. After a moment, Eileen looked up again and continued listening.

Jeff told Eileen how his church, and co-workers had been a source of blessing and encouragement to him in his grief. He finished by telling Eileen that, even though his life had been difficult, and he felt like he had been living in a dark and cold world, he had much for which to be thankful.

After a while, Jeff looked up and said; "Okay Eileen, I have shared with you, about my life. I would like to know about your life."

"My life has been completely different from yours." Eileen spoke with a distant look in her eyes. "I grew up in a single parent home. My mother was a lawyer and made very good money. As far as a father, I don't remember my mother ever mentioning my father's name. All that she told me was that he was a man who had been in her life one summer for a few months, and the result of that was me. The man had been a drifter and had left her pregnant and alone. She had been tempted to have an abortion, but had decided against it. She had been brought up differently, and had qualms about getting an abortion. I have to say that when I was kidnapped and alone, I went back over my life and I wished that she had had an abortion when she carried me. At least then I would have been out of my misery."

Eileen continued. "When I was a teenager, my mother was too busy for me. But she bought me lots of stuff. I loved going shopping with my friends and we would just have a blast. But I also loved going to high school, and I gave it all I had. I wanted to be good at what I did. My mother was good at what she did, and I wanted to emulate her. She was my hero. When I was in grade twelve, I got hooked up with a popular guy from the high school basketball team. He said he loved me and I, of course, believed him. We started hanging out and we thought we would get married right out of high school. He made a lot of promises about what he was going to buy me, what he was doing to do for me and so on. My mother warned me about him though, and it got between us. Mother tried to tell me to test him. She said if this guy was real, he would look out for me, protect me and make no demands of me. But I took his side over mom's advice. I kept going out with him, to my mother's great disappointment. About three months into our relationship, I realized that I was pregnant. I knew he was the father because I had had no one else. But I didn't dare tell my mother. I was eighteen, and gave the pregnancy some serious thought. It was hard for me."

Jeff looked at Eileen, with a seriousness in his eyes that didn't escape Eileen's notice.

"Well, initially it was hard for me," Eileen continued. "I was confused and was not sure where to go, or who to talk to. I needed advice. But I didn't want my mother to find out, for fear of what it would do to her. She was working hard, putting money away for her retirement, and my college education. I thought of my mother, and how often she had talked about how being pregnant had interfered with her life. That was when I made my decision." Eileen paused again.

Jeff seemed visibly moved by what he expected would come next. But he asked it anyway. "And what was that decision?"

"My decision was to terminate the pregnancy," Eileen said. "I realized what a mistake I had made in trusting this basketball player. It dawned on me that he had no intentions of keeping a single one of his promises to me. I don't think that he was intentionally lying. He was just saying what he needed to say to get access to my life for his own pleasure. I think to him I was just a fish on the end of a fisherman's line, to be caught and filleted. To him, I was just an object, a trophy. I was very hurt and disappointed in him. So I decided to end the pregnancy. I was determined that what had happened to my mother would not happen to me."

Jeff was looking down at his food as he listened to Eileen talk. She noticed his silence, and his increasing mental distance from what she was saying.

"Is something wrong Jeff?" she asked. "Something I said?"

"It's just hard to explain. I guess we are from such opposite ends of the spectrum that we see things with completely different world views."

"What do you mean?"

"Sorry, continue your story, Eileen. I am interested in hearing what you have to say."

Eileen was now uncertain as to where this discussion could lead. She didn't want to distance herself from Jeff. That she was sure of. But she was also not sure if he was ready to hear what she had to say. She didn't want this dinner together to lead to a negative exchange of ideas. In some ways, she felt very much like a stranger to him still. But at the same time, she felt safe with him.

She continued. "When I realized how much it cost my mother to provide for, and take care of, a child as a single mother, I decided not to go that route. I did the math, added up the time required to care for a child, and knew I was not able to be a mother and make a living at the same time, or pursue my dreams. So, I decided to end the pregnancy for the benefit of both myself, and the fetus. It was better that way. At least, no one would have to suffer."

Eileen stopped talking and was continuing with her meal. Jeff felt he had to interject something at this point.

"You say, 'benefit for both yourself and the fetus.' I'm sure it must have been very difficult for you to make that choice, and part of me wants to sympathize with you in your situation. But you are talking about a human life here ... uh ... how do you feel about ending a pregnancy?"

Eating, Eileen waited to respond, and then spoke. "Well," she, responded hesitantly, "I think it's just like stopping something that has a potential to turn out badly, before it does. For me, to have a child would have been bad. But, from what you tell me, not having a baby was what was bad for you and Faye. So, I guess it all depends."

"If you really believe that," Jeff began, "where would you draw the line? I have so many questions when it comes to this topic. Being a man, I can't speak from a woman's perspective, and I'm sure I don't know all the answers. But, from what I have thought about, and listened to, it seems to me we are talking about human life here, are we not? And if that is the case, who is to decide when a human life has rights, and deserves protection? Where do we draw the line? Is a fetus not a baby?"

Eileen stopped eating, and responded, a bit forcefully. "Jeff, are you implying that I killed a baby? I didn't do anything illegal. I simply tried to avoid a bad situation, and I didn't want something bad to get worse. That was all. But if that's the way you put it – well sometimes death is the answer to a problem, is it not? Think of what would have happened had you not killed Oscar Ritchie. Both of us would be dead by now if you had not stepped in. Not only that, how many others might have gotten killed as well?

Jeff responded slowly. "Killing Oscar was not my goal, or intention. I felt I was forced to kill him to stop the killing. It seems we are talking about different things here. When I shot and killed Oscar, yes, I ended his life. But I ended a lot more. I ended a serial killer's killing spree. As much as I believe life is sacred, someone had to stop this killer and, unfortunately, it was Oscar himself who determined it."

Jeff paused, and then continued. "In my upbringing, I was taught that to end a life, regardless of the circumstances is wrong. If the circumstances are difficult, or stressful, that doesn't mean that a life should be ended. That is what I was taught and I believe that. Everyone has value and should be given protection regardless of what stage of life they are in. Even Oscar, as far as the value of his life was concerned. My people, among whom I grew up, will not all agree with me that I did the right thing by killing Oscar. I am sometimes not even totally sure myself where I stand with what I did. But to do nothing would be a more cowardly thing than to take the actions that I took. But killing a serial killer, and ending the life of an unborn child, well ... that, to me, is a night and day difference. Killing Oscar was ending a fountain of evil that would perhaps destroy and kill who knows how many other innocent lives."

Jeff waited, as if collecting and sorting his thoughts, and giving Eileen time to digest what he had just said, and then continued. "When it comes to an unborn child, things are different. I mean, a little baby inside the womb, what has the child done, except gotten in the adult's way by the choice of the adults, when they decided to have sex together. Not only that, the little baby is totally dependent on the hosting womb for life and protection. And the baby can't argue for itself. The baby can't in any way request protection and sustenance. When protection and sustenance, and even life, is denied the little human being growing inside the mother's body, for the simple reason that there might not be money to feed another mouth, or that having the baby will interfere with plans, what do you call that? The child is being made to pay the bill for the actions of the adults. I see it as the cost or consequences for the adult's choices being put on the child. The child has to pay, with its blood, the bill for the adults' decision."

It was immediately clear to Jeff that his words had left Eileen deeply disturbed and shaken. He had said too much, too soon. He had not intended to call her a baby killer, but he realized that this was what she may have understood he meant, no matter how good or well intentioned her motives might have been in ending the pregnancy. For a moment, Jeff wished he had said nothing.

"I'm sorry, Eileen." Jeff continued quickly. "I didn't mean to disturb you like that. Let me just finish by saying that my view is that, in giving my life, I find that I preserve my life. Giving up my security, for the security of another, is the highest goal in life. As I meet the needs of others, I find my own needs are met. But, if I short change someone else for my own sake, then I am, in the end, robbing myself of the very blessings I could be enjoying. We all have a need for meaning, purpose and fulfilment, in different ways. My view is that I find my purpose, and destiny, by giving myself to the needs of others. In putting the needs of others before my own, I find a true sense of worth in myself. If I become inward, and self-focused, and start controlling the lives of others for my own benefit, I become demanding and controlling. And, in the process, I find I am destroying the lives of those I try to control and rule over. Not only that, I destroy my own life too, the very thing I am trying to protect at the expense of others. Really, it is a question of direction. We all try to find ways to fill our lives with what gives us meaning. Some just do it by taking from others, some do it by giving to others."

Eileen sat on her side of the table, looking at him as a student looks at teacher, who has said something that seems to make sense, but the student has never heard before. "I'm not sure I follow," Eileen said slowly. "How can that work? It didn't work for my mother, and how would it have worked for me?"

Jeff responded. "You say it didn't work for your mother. That is a subjective statement, Eileen. Who interprets an event? You have no way of knowing how your mother's life would have been different if your mother had done with you as you think she should have. Often in life, the very things that we think we cannot do without, or that we think we need to steer clear of, are the very things that we need to keep us grounded, and on a firm foundation."

Jeff realized that they had finished their plates, and the waitress had already filled their coffees a few times.

Eileen spoke up. "I have never heard this kind of stuff before. I have to process this."

"I hope that I have not caused you more pain than you have already been through. My desire is to see you do well. My concern for you is not based on whether or not you agree with my beliefs, or see things the way I do. I only want to see you become what God destined you to be."

Eileen didn't speak for a while. It was clear that she had gotten more than she had bargained for when she wanted to go for dinner with Jeff.

Jeff sensed that it was time to close off the evening. "Eileen, let me get the bill, and I will walk you to your car."

"Thank you."

As they left the diner, she turned to Jeff, and looked up at him. "Jeff, I don't know why I am saying this, but even though we are so different, I have to tell you that I am not feeling judged by you. I think you have been honest with me. That means a lot. I have to say that I am searching, and I think you can help me."

Inwardly Jeff breathed a sigh of relief. "Well, let's meet again sometime. Anytime is good with me. Just let me know, and we can talk some more."

Eileen got into her car and, on her way home, and later in bed, her mind continued going over what had happened at the diner. She was grateful, in her heart, that she had been in the company of this strong tall man. In a strange sort of way, she felt secure in his presence. He had not made any moves or said anything to her that gave her reason not to trust him. Tonight, her mind was not sleepy. In the last number of days she had been through too much, experienced too much and had seen too much, to get any sleep just now. She was not sure what to make of Jeff. He had made deep, soul-piercing, penetrating comments and questions about life. It was as if he lived on a different plane, somewhere where her soul yearned to be. He had put things into a perspective that she had never even considered. She knew he was implying that she had killed her unborn baby. "What if he's right?" she thought.

Her mind continued thinking as the night hours wore on. She could not shake this man. It was as if life, to him, was something so special that it superseded everything else, and everything had to square with it. And if, whatever it was in your life, didn't add to the value of it, then that thing was expendable. She could tell from listening to him, and observing him, that he held deep convictions. "Like praying before eating, for instance," she thought. She had heard of people with such weird notions, but had never thought she would one day be rescued, and later be drawn to, a person like that. It occurred to her that it had been to her advantage that he held the values that he did. If his values were selfish, who knows what he would have done when he had stumbled on the van, and heard her cries for help. In her mind, she shuddered again at the thought of what would have happened had he not found her, and made her his responsibility. Her mind went to their conversation about life, killing, and making choices. She could not figure out what was up with him about protecting the unborn. For her, she had always believed that it was a woman's right to decide what was best for her body. Never had she heard the idea that it was not about what was right for one person only, but what exercising that right would bring, or cost, the other person. In her mind, she had not seen it like that, but it was obvious to her that Jeff did. She realized that if what Jeff was saying had merit, that made her a selfish person, at the least, a person who would deny the rights of a helpless child to support her own desires. She knew in her heart that she would like to hear more about this topic, even though she didn't agree with it. There was something here that seemed to bring some light to her heart that she had never seen or felt before. Time would tell. In the early hours of the morning, her mind drifted off to sleep.

Chapter 15

The next few weeks were very busy for Jeff as he busied himself at work, getting ready for the Christmas holidays. His foreman had a lot of orders that needed to be completed before Christmas. Jeff was hoping that, once the Christmas rush was over, he would have a more leisurely pace at work again. He was hoping he might have some time in February or March to go south for a week or two. In his mind, he was still thinking of Eileen. He still sometimes thought of Faye at night, but not in the same way he used to. In his heart, he knew that, in some ways, he would miss her forever, but it was beginning to look different. His heart was healing and the pain was leaving him. For that, he was grateful. In his mind, he was planning for another visit with Eileen. He realized that he felt a lot more insecure about himself in this area, of building a relationship with Eileen, than he had realized. He decided he was not going to call her yet. He was not completely sure of his motives. It was not that it would be wrong or anything but, in his heart, he felt he needed to let these thoughts mature a bit more, before he acted on them. For now, he would just patiently wait and busy himself with his work.

In the early part of December, he received a letter from the Police department. His heart skipped a beat as he opened the official letter, and skimmed over its contents. It was regarding the death of Oscar Ritchie. It stated that the police department had done a detailed investigation and had ruled the death of Oscar Ritchie a result of self-defence on the part of Jeff Nolan, for himself, as well as Eileen Benson. The crown had decided that there would be no charges against him. The story that he had told the police, and the one that Eileen Benson had told them, matched. That, together with the forensic evidence found in the cave, was enough to establish that Oscar was a serial killer, and had simply run out of luck, thanks to the courage and bravery of Jeff Nolan. Jeff was relieved that it was over. There would be no repercussions against him from the law, and he didn't have to fear anything from anyone else. As far as the other remains that had been recovered, the police were looking further into the matter and would continue to investigate those particular crimes. For Jeff, life was settling back to a routine.

Just before Christmas, one Friday evening, the phone rang. It was Eileen. "Hi Jeff," she said cheerily on the other end. "How have you been?"

"Oh, same old, same old, I guess," he responded. "But happy to hear your voice again. How are things?"

"Actually, that's why I called, Jeff. I have been busy with work, but I want to come out on Sunday again and see you. I would like to come early enough to go to your church with you ... if that's okay?"

"Why, of course, just come over. Church is at 9:30 am. We would love to have you. And, if you want, we can go to my place for lunch afterwards, or we can go out and get something."

"Either way is fine with me, Jeff. I have some more things I would like to talk about, and would not mind hearing your thoughts."

"It would be nice of you to come to my church, and you will be very welcome." Jeff assured her. He was actually looking forward to their talks.

"Okay then, see you at church on Sunday, at 9:30." She hung up, and Jeff held the receiver for a few moments. "So," he thought. "She has called again. She is interested in something. That's for sure."

Jeff's mind began to relive the time he had met Eileen for the first time. She seemed so different now. Now, it was looking as if this young woman was taking an active interest in his faith. "Would that not be something?" Jeff thought. "First, I get to be there to save her life, and now I may be the conduit through which she will find real joy, purpose and meaning in life again. But not only that," Jeff's mind went on. "I have to be honest with myself; I am developing feelings for this young woman.'

Sunday morning, Jeff was up early and ready for church ahead of time. He had given Eileen directions to the church. He was there well ahead of time in his truck. He found that he was excited at seeing Eileen; looking forward to it, a bit like a little boy looks forward to Christmas. Eileen arrived just before 9:30. Jeff got out of his truck and walked over to where she had parked her car. She was just getting out.

"Good morning, Eileen. Good to see you!" Jeff exclaimed. "Do you want to walk in with me?"

"Sure, thanks."

Together, they walked side by side, as two friends, toward the church. Jeff's mind was not really on the service. This was the first time in years that he had walked another woman into church. The last time, it had been Faye. But, as he walked

Eileen in, he felt as if there was almost no trace of longing for Faye, in his heart. It was not that he had forgotten her. He realized that he was finally healing from the loss he had felt when she passed away. Inside the building, Jeff picked out a seat that was close to the middle of the rows of pews. He escorted Eileen toward one of the middle pews, and followed her and sat down. He was consciously aware that there were people noticing he had a woman with him. "Oh well," he told himself, "this means nothing more than that I brought a friend to church."

It was a regular worship service, with Pastor Raymond as the speaker. When it was his turn to get up and speak, he welcomed the congregation, and made special mention and notice of the visitor that had come with Jeff Nolan. Jeff hoped that Eileen would not feel too self-conscious in this small church, where everyone knew everyone.

Pastor Raymond spoke, that Sunday morning, on the meaning of God's gift for mankind. He stated that because God loved humanity so much, he went all out and became one of them, so he could reach out to them, teach them his ways on how to live for each other, and love one another. He gave a brief description of the birth of Jesus, and how that birth was the beginning of a journey that Jesus went to both joyfully, but also at great risk and, in the end, was killed because popular and national opinion turned against him. Pastor Raymond explained how it was through the birth of Jesus that we had been given an insight into God's love for us. And he explained that it was through the death and resurrection of Christ that we have been given eternal life, if we accept his gift of grace in faith.

The worship service ended and Jeff and Eileen made their way to the door. Pastor Raymond, with his wife Betty, were standing by the door as Jeff and Eileen walked out. They greeted Eileen warmly, and thanked her for coming.

Jeff walked Eileen to her car, and stood there with her for a few moments. "Eileen," Jeff began, "I was thinking. How about if you take your car, and we drive over to my place, and we both head to town together for lunch? Would you be interested?"

"Sure, I will follow you," Eileen responded, as she opened the car door and got in.

Jeff got into his truck and drove the short distance to his house from the church. At his house, Eileen parked her car and together they headed off to Forest Hill. It was getting close to the Holidays and with the presence of Christmas decorations everywhere, things were in a festive mood. On the road to town, he asked Eileen where she liked to eat. "Do you have any special preference?"

"No, I'm fine with pretty much anything. It was your idea, so you choose," she said, with a twinkle in her eyes and a cheerful smile.

"Okay, I like a place called Granny's diner, how does that sound?"

"Like I said Jeff, you choose. That sounds fine with me."

The Sunday crowd was not very big this afternoon. Jeff and Eileen were seated in a quiet booth in the southwest corner. It was a pleasant area with sun beams coming in through the window. Eileen was sitting in the sun, taking in the sights of the restaurant. Jeff observed her quietly. It seemed to him he had gotten quite an insight into this young woman's heart. She had shared quite a bit with him, her experiences in life, how she had handled them, and how they had affected her.

A waitress came by, offering to get their drink order. Jeff and Eileen both chose coffee as they received their menus and looked over what was being offered that day. Jeff picked a half rack of ribs and Eileen chose fish and chips.

As they sat sipping coffee, and waiting for food, it was an opportunity to just be in each others' presence. After a few moments, Eileen spoke up. "Jeff," she began, "I have heard a lot of what your pastor spoke on this morning. But I have to honestly say that I have never paid attention to it, or had an interest in it until recently, in the last while since I met you, that is. I remember what you have told me about living a good life, having a relationship with Jesus and so on, but I still have a few questions."

"That's okay," Jeff replied. "I hope you are not making your decisions based on any type of pressure from anyone."

"No, Jeff. I have been thinking about you a lot, what you believe and what you stand for. I think my mind is made up. I'm just not sure how to make the change; I mean how to become a follower of Christ." As much as he tried to hide his excitement, it was not totally possible. Eileen noticed it. "You seem excited."

"Well, it's just that, uh ... well, I am excited, Eileen. I had not guessed that you would make up your mind so soon. I am very excited for you. If you have thought this through, and are serious, I would be most delighted to hear that you have made up your mind in this matter.

"If becoming a follower of Jesus is what I have heard you say it is, and what your pastor says it is, then I want to," Eileen said. "I am serious about this."

"Good," Jeff replied. "I would like to be the first to hear your testimony on that commitment. But before you do make that decision, I want to know if you understand what you are doing. It is not an easy thing. It may be simple, but it is both a life-long, and eternal, decision. Are you aware of that?"

"Yes, I am aware," she answered pleasantly. "If I understand it correctly, God came to earth in human form, and showed us how to live. He enabled us to be his children, if we believe in his name. I think I read that in the gospel of John in the first chapter. But then, on the flip side, it takes me everything I have to follow him, right? I mean like Jesus telling the people that unless they are willing to deny themselves and take up their cross and follow him, they cannot be his disciples, right? I mean, it's like Jesus gave it all, one hundred percent, and for this to work, for it to be real, his followers too have to give a hundred percent. Is that correct?"

"Yes, Eileen, that's it! You got it!" Jeff was excited.

"Okay, how do I make it, uh ... I guess, make it official, Jeff?" Eileen asked.

"Well, you just make that comittment in your heart and say it," Jeff responded enthusiastically. "I mean, just pray to God, right now, and tell him that you are repenting of your sin, and giving your life to him completely. Give him control of your life and surrender to him. That's it."

Eileen looked at Jeff with eyes as sincere as those of a little school girl. "I'm ready Jeff," Eileen said simply. "Will you help me?"

It was almost more than Jeff had expected. Here was a person whom he felt had made a sincere decision. It was now his privilege to walk alongside her in her journey, and be her encouragement and support. He spoke. "Okay Eileen, we have about ten to fifteen minutes to wait before our food gets here. Let's just bow our heads, and you tell Jesus what you want to tell him about yourself, and how you want to live for him. That's it."

Jeff bowed his head and waited for Eileen to pray. She began, hesitantly, but sure. "Jesus, I have heard about you, many times, but never really understood you. In my upbringing, you were not a part of my life, or my mother's life. I only learned to live for myself. I lived life for myself, thinking I was good. I didn't know I was missing so much until I met Jeff. Thank you for showing me a new way, of hope and life. I just want to say that I am sorry for my way of life, for the many ways in which I disobeyed and lived so selfishly, for all the wrong things I have done. I ask for your forgiveness. I just want to say to you that, as of today, I am turning from my life of selfish living, what your word calls sin, and I am giving myself to you for good. Thank you for giving your life for me on the cross, and paying for my sins. I want to follow you, as I have seen Jeff do. Thank you for what you have done for me. Thank you. Amen."

Jeff raised his head and looked at Eileen. He could not hide the tears in his eyes, as he looked into Eileen's. He saw, in her eyes, tears of joy, and a sparkle and lightness that he had not seen before. His mind went back to the day when he saw her the first time in the van, shivering in cold and fear, captive to the kidnapper, and later, how together with her in the van, she had been mad at him for believing in prayer. How she had changed in such a short time.

Eileen returned his look with a silent smile, and tears of joy in her eyes. Jeff was at a loss for what to say. Silently, he took his cup of coffee and took a sip.

Jeff spoke slowly. "Eileen, you have been rescued twice now. First, when you were kidnapped, God used me to find you and, through my hand, he freed you. And now, he has rescued you from the fear of death, and the worries of life. I'm happy for you."

"Thank you Jeff," Eileen responded, quietly. "I know what you may be thinking. I was mad at you for being a Christian and all, when you found me, but I realize now what God did. I said, back then, that God couldn't possibly be a God of love, because he let something this bad happen, I mean the kidnapping. But now I see a bigger part of the picture. All that evil, that day, was used by God to bring me to him. Isn't that amazing?"

The waitress came with their food and set down the plates. "Is there anything else you need," she asked.

"No thanks. We are fine." Jeff said.

Eileen reached out and touched Jeff's hand. "This time, allow me to say thanks for the food." She said with a smile.

"Fine by me," Jeff replied. He liked the touch of her hand on his. Even though his hand had been in contact with Eileen's before, it had been different. His heart rate went up as her hand rested on his. It was like an electric pulse raced through him.

After Eileen thanked God for the food, Jeff ate his rack of ribs with a feeling of joy. His heart danced with a feeling of youthfulness that he had not felt in years.

They finished their meal and, together, they drove back to Jeff's place. " If you want, we can just stay at my house for a while, or we can go and visit some of my friends," Jeff commented.

"Thanks, but I think, for today, I will go home. Thanks for taking me up on my request to come to your church, and also now, for inviting me in. But I have someone I want to talk to about my decision. I think I would like to go and tell Ruby what I have experienced. I would like to share with her my happiness."

"Good idea. But let me ask you, is Ruby a Christian?"

Eileen paused. "No, I don't believe she is. She is a good woman, but I have never heard her make any comment or reference to her faith. No. I don't think she is a Christian. But why do you ask?"

"Well," Jeff began. "I want to encourage you to do what you said, and share with her what you have experienced. But, I also want you to be aware that not all people are excited about faith in God, or a relationship with Jesus," Jeff finished, with a slight twinkle in his eye.

Instantly, Eileen remembered. "I see. You are right. I remember my first reaction to you, when I saw a real demonstration of faith for the first time. Thanks for giving me a heads up. But I will do what I saw you do, Jeff. I will just follow through with what I know is right, regardless of what Ruby, or anyone else, will say."

"Good. That's the Spirit," Jeff replied. "On another note," he continued, "Christmas is in a few days. Are you doing anything special during the holidays?"

"No, nothing other than wanting to go and see my mom. Right after the holidays, I will be back to work. Why, did you have something in mind?"

"I was just thinking," Jeff said, "how about us getting together again for a visit soon? You are a new Christian, and you need to connect with other Christians. Do you have a church you would like to go to?"

"I think I will just go to your church," Eileen responded. "I have observed your life, and if your church is like you are, then it must be a good church. Would that be okay with you, I mean, me going to your church?"

"Why, of course, of course. It would be an honour to have you."

"Well then, that's settled. I will see again next Sunday." With that, Eileen got into her car and was off.

Jeff walked into his small house, almost as if he was walking on air. He found it hard to believe what he had experienced today. He had witnessed a woman rescued for the second time in her life. In his heart, he had to admit that he had developed feelings for her. On the one hand, he was almost a bit upset with himself. This was all so soon. But, on the other hand, he realized that, if this was the way God was leading him, he had nothing to worry about.

Chapter 16

Next Sunday, as Jeff drove to church, he was not sure what to expect of himself. Should he walk Eileen in again, or should he just pretend not to notice her? He decided he was going to befriend her, given the fact that it was only her second time in his church, and she didn't really know anyone yet.

When he drove into the parking lot, he pulled into his normal parking spot and looked for Eileen's little Ford Focus. She was not there yet. He decided to wait. He looked at his watch, and realized he was at least ten minutes early.

At exactly nine twenty-five, the little Focus drove into the parking lot. As she pulled into a parking spot, Jeff watched for her to get out of her car. As she got out, he got out of his truck and walked in the direction of the church door, making sure he would meet up with her there. As she neared the entrance, Jeff walked up beside her and greeted her.

"Good morning Eileen! How are you?"

"Good morning Jeff, I'm fine thank you."

"You mind if I walk you in?"

"No, not at all."

Together they walked in and sat down close to the spot they had sat the last time. It was a normal service, as usual, with the congregation singing, Pastor Raymond preaching, a prayer time, and a closing song. As they were making their way out of the service, Eileen whispered to Jeff. "I would like to meet your pastor couple."

"Good, lets see if we can meet with them."

As they walked toward the entrance, Pastor Raymond and his wife Betty were greeting and shaking hands with the people as they were leaving. Jeff walked up to Pastor Raymond. "Good morning Pastor Raymond, Betty, would you have a moment to talk with us after the people have filed out?"

"Sure, of course. I will be available in a few minutes." Pastor Raymond responded. Jeff and Eileen waited in the foyer and, in a few minutes, Pastor Raymond and Betty walked over to them.

"Hi Jeff, Eileen; it's good to see you," Pastor Raymond began. "How are you doing?" He and his wife both smiled cheerfully as they greeted Jeff and Eileen.

"We are doing well, thank you," Jeff responded. "We would like to see if it would be possible for Eileen and myself to visit with you?"

"Sure, when would you like? We are free this afternoon. Could we invite you over?"

Jeff looked at Eileen. She was the first to respond. "I think that would be great. What do you think?" she asked looking at Jeff.

"I'm good with it," Jeff responded. "Let's do that then."

"So, we will see you later this afternoon."

"Okay, does three o'clock sound good?" Jeff asked.

"That sounds good to us," Pastor Raymond answered.

On the way out, Jeff looked at Eileen and suggested that they leave her car in the parking lot, take his truck, and headed out to Jeff's place for lunch, and spend a few hours together until it was time to head back to the pastor couple's house. Pastor Raymond and Betty lived next door to the church, and there was no need for them to use both vehicles.

As Jeff and Eileen drove together to his house, Jeff's mind was thinking of how fast life had changed for him in less than two months. Most of his days for the last four years had been dark and lonely. But now, with Eileen coming into his life, it seemed as if spring time had arrived. The greatest joy for him so far was the fact that she had made a faith decision in her life, and that she had chosen to attend his church.

After driving for a few minutes, Eileen looked over to him. "What are you thinking?" It seemed to Jeff as if she was trying to strike up a conversation.

"Oh, I was just thinking about how fast life has changed for me. You know, I have experienced so many blessings recently that I still can't quite comprehend it all." He looked over at Eileen, as he finished his sentence. "But why were you asking?"

His sense had been right. She wanted to talk.

She began. "I have been thinking about a lot of things lately. Remember on that Saturday when you first found me, how I berated you in that van for your faith in God? Well, since I have given my life to Christ, I have been remembering some things." She paused.

Jeff looked over in her direction, waiting for her to continue. "What have you been remembering?" he asked, not knowing where this was going to go.

"What I said to you in the van was wrong. I should have not been so thoughtless. God has been convicting me of some things I need to make right" Eileen responded, with some emotion in her voice.

Jeff waited a moment, and commented. "Eileen, you don't need to be afraid to talk about what happened that day. A lot of things happened that day. I know it was a very difficult time for you, and me as well. I have tried to forget about some of the stuff that happened, but if you would, refresh my mind. Are you referring to something specific?"

It was clear that Eileen's mind was heavy as she spoke. "When I lashed out at you for believing in prayer, when I ridiculed you for believing in God, that he has a plan and all that, I was wrong. I need your forgiveness."

Jeff turned to her and, in a gentle voice, responded. "I forgave you right then, as you said those words. I looked deeper and what I saw was hurt, pain and fear in your life. I never held it against you, for even a moment."

"Thank you," she smiled. Her eyes were glistening with tears that were ready to spill over. She continued. "Well, as it has turned out, that kidnapping has turned out to be something good. I find it so amazing. I would have never believed that the darkest thing to happen to me in my life would turn out to be the turning point to something so beautiful. It was when I was destined to die, that God sent you to rescue me."

"I remember that too," Jeff responded. "I saw then how deep in pain and fear you were. I am just glad that you have made the choice to give your life to God, and to follow God's principles for your life from here on. I think that so far has given me the greatest joy." He looked over at her and smiled.

They were pulling up to Jeff's house. He made some quick mental decisions about what he was going to cook for lunch. "Eileen, how are you with hamburgers and chips?"

"Fine by me, if you are cooking," Eileen smiled pleasantly.

"Okay, burgers and chips it is."

Jeff had lived by himself so long that he had forgotten what it was like to eat together with a woman in his house. He took some beef patties and slid them into the little toaster oven and put it on high. With the winter weather, it was too cold to barbecue anything outside.

"They should be done in a little while," Jeff commented. "Meantime, why don't you just make yourself comfortable, and we will eat as soon as the burgers are finished.

Eileen walked around the small house, and looked around. He didn't have many possessions. That was obvious. He had a shelf with some books on it, and a few pictures. A few of them were pictures of Jeff and Faye as a couple.

Jeff noticed Eileen looking at the pictures. He finished setting the table and walked over to her. She was looking at a picture of him and Faye.

Presently, Eileen spoke. "She was beautiful."

Jeff was not sure how to respond. It almost seemed awkward. "Yes, Faye was beautiful. But something has been happening to me, Eileen," he added. "In the last while, the pain is not what it used to be, and I have come to a healing point in all of this. As good as our times together were, I believe I am turning to a new chapter in my life. I have come to realize that Faye would not want me to continue my life feeling lonely and isolated. I have decided to move on. And I know that I would have her blessing."

Jeff stood beside Eileen, and put his arm around her. She looked up at him. "I could never replace Faye," she said, as she looked at Jeff with searching eyes.

"You are not replacing Faye," Jeff responded softly, as he looked into Eileen's eyes. "Faye and I were God's gift to each other for a time. God took her from me. That was his doing. I don't know why, and will never know why. But I trust his hand. Now, I believe God may have something for you and me together, which we are, perhaps, just discovering." Jeff look continued to look at Eileen with tender eyes.

Eileen blushed. “I have been feeling this for some time now, but didn’t want to rush anything. I was wondering if you felt the same thing.”

“I was feeling the same thing,” Jeff responded. “But I didn’t want to rush anything either”

The oven timer went off and interrupted their thoughts. “I think the burgers are done,” Jeff commented. “Here, lets sit down and eat.”

They sat down together at the table, and Jeff gave thanks for the food. The table seemed sparsely set with just the beef patties, some buns, slices of cheese and tomatoes, and the chips. “I’m sorry that I’m not much of a cook.”

“Jeff,” Eileen commented, gently, “Don’t say that. Remember at the campfire the first night, when you rescued me, you put some canned meat and corn into a small aluminium dish and you said something similar? I have to say that I think you should not apologize for the food. I think you are doing fine.”

“Sorry,” Jeff replied. “I know better than to say such things.” Jeff’s mind went to Eileen’s comment earlier, in the church, when she had said she wanted to see the pastor couple. He wanted to ask her about that. “Eileen, in our visit to Pastor Raymond and Betty this afternoon, do you have any special things you want to talk about?”

“I do,” she said. “I would like to become a member of your church. I feel I need the connection of other believers. Of course, I have you,” she said with a twinkle, “but I want fellowship with different believers too. What would it take to become a member?

“Well, what it takes is simply making a statement to the congregation that you have decided to live for Jesus, that you have repented of your sins, and now want to identify with God’s people.”

"Is that it?" Eileen asked.

"Pretty much yes, except you will be expected to participate in church and so on."

"That is pretty much what I want to visit about this afternoon."

"That won't be difficult then, I can assure you." Jeff responded.

Their conversation floated around to work, and its daily challenges. After lunch, Jeff and Eileen sat around the table, drinking coffee for a while,, until it was time to head back to Pastor Raymond and Betty's house. At two forty five Jeff said, "I think we can head out to Pastor Raymond's house now.

The pastor couple welcomed Jeff and Eileen warmly into their home. "How was your noon hour?" Pastor Raymond asked.

"Good, we spent the time at my place, and visited, and now we are here," Jeff responded.

"Let's sit down in the living room, and you make yourselves comfortable," Betty said, pleasantly.

As they got settled in, after a time of light conversation, Eileen changed the subject of discussion. "You may have been wondering what my reason was for requesting a visit. Well, I have been doing a lot of thinking in the last number of weeks. As I am sure you are aware, I was kidnapped last November, and Jeff happened to come by, and rescued me, I didn't have any peace after that episode. And it was, in large part, due to Jeff here. I watched him that day, closer than I have ever watched any person, ever. When he rescued me and I was free to go, something didn't seem right. I felt I owed him something for it. But, as the days went by, I realized that Jeff was the way he was because of something else in his life. He had something I wanted, a faith in God, and I didn't know what that meant. As time went on, I realized with increasing conviction that what Jeff had was real, and it was something I not only wanted, but needed. Since then, I have made the decision to be a follower of Jesus. My question to you is, what I would have to do to be a part of your church?"

Pastor Raymond had been listening carefully. "Really, Eileen, You are already a member of the church of Jesus Christ. All that you are now asking is to be a local member here, this particular body of believers. That is easily arranged. If you want to be a member, and serve with your gifts and talents in this church, we can arrange for you to share your testimony with our congregation, and tell us what God has done in your life. Then, we can baptize you and receive you as a member in our church. It's really quite that simple. And, might I add, I am very glad that you have made this decision in your life and, also, that you have decided to fellowship here. However, I must say, I think that perhaps Jeff here is a drawing card?" He finished his last sentence with an easy smile.

"Yes, Jeff has been, and is, a drawing card, I admit," Eileen agreed pleasantly, giving a quick glance in Jeff's direction. "But we are not taking anything fast here. We want to see what God will do, and where he takes us. For now, that is where we are at." With that, she looked over at Jeff as if waiting for him to respond.

"That's right," Jeff added. "Eileen and I do have feelings for each other. We also both realize that we are adults, and we want to take this responsibly. We are not rushing into anything, and realize that we are dependent on Gods' grace in our lives.

"Back to this matter of becoming a member," Pastor Raymond started again, "When did you have in mind, Eileen?"

"I was thinking, perhaps, some time in the next several weeks. How would that be?"

"That sounds fine to me. I will make sure that we arrange a Sunday morning when we can do this."

After an hour of visiting, Jeff and Eileen decided to get ready to leave.

Pastor Raymond and Betty escorted them to the door, and thanked them for coming. Together, Jeff and Eileen walked to his truck, and drove over to the church parking lot next door.

Pastor Raymond watched them leave and then turned to his wife. "Well, what do you know? It seems our Jeff will come around again. He has found love again and, who knows, we may just get to do a wedding for Jeff and Eileen in the near future, maybe even as soon as spring time is here."

Chapter 17

January and February were cold months, as Jeff spent his working days at the trailer factory. But, in his heart, a warm spring breeze was moving steadily, every day. The ice in his soul that had been there for four long years was pretty much gone.

In early February, Eileen had been given the opportunity to share her testimony of faith with the congregation at his church. The small congregation at Hope Fellowship Church had been very warm, and welcoming of Eileen. It was an emotional experience for Eileen to open up in front of a group of people, and share her heart with them.

Eileen shared with them, everything she had already told Jeff, even speaking about her abortion and how remorseful she now was over her actions. In her testimony, Eileen became very emotional as she related how, as a real estate agent, she had been lured into showing a house to a serial killer, and then was kidnapped. She had been angry at herself, and then later at her rescuer, whom she later found out was a believer in God. She also shared how Jeff had patiently stood his ground, and kept an open heart toward her, in spite of all her anger and bitterness. It had been because of God's love, living through Jeff, that she had warmed up to faith in Jesus, and she had made that faith her own.

After sharing her story, she simply stated that it was her desire to be part of this congregation and join their fellowship. The congregation applauded. Next, Pastor Raymond got up and asked Eileen to come forward, to answer a few questions, before baptizing her. First, he asked her if it was her desire to serve Christ in this local body of believers. She answered in the affirmative. Next, he asked her if it was her wish, upon her confession of faith, to receive water baptism. Again, she answered, "yes." After she had been baptized, she was welcomed as a member into the church.

That Sunday was etched into Jeff's mind. What had happened to Eileen had done something to him too. After her baptism, and reception into membership, it seemed to Jeff that he had gotten back his feeling of belonging. He felt at home again.

At his work, the co-workers had been making comments about how Jeff was his old self again. Even though most of his co-workers were not Christians, they were still happy, that life was turning around for him.

In the evenings, Jeff noticed that his heart was more and more focused on Eileen, with each passing week. He realized that he loved Eileen with his heart and mind, completely. As the weeks flowed on, Jeff and Eileen spent more and more time together.

One evening, after coming home from work to his small house, he decided that he would ask Eileen for her hand in marriage. He had lived alone long enough. He had his dogs, but they were not people. He was still alone, in their presence. He wanted someone to give himself to, someone to love and serve.

One Friday night in February, Jeff had decided that he would take Eileen out for a dinner in Forest Hill. This was not going to be just a normal dinner. It was going to be a special evening. He had purchased an engagement ring for Eileen.

Jeff had made arrangements to pick Eileen up at her apartment at six. It seemed that he could not wait till it was time to punch out and go home that day. The day seemed to drag on. Finally, the buzzer sounded and he was on his way out. He quickly rushed home, took care of his dogs, showered, dressed up in his formal best, and went back to town. Then he drove up to Eileen's apartment, and knocked on the door. Ruby Miller answered it.

"Oh hi, you must be Jeff." Ruby seemed a bit surprised.

"Yes," Jeff replied. "I am here to pick up Eileen. I don't know if she told you."

"Yes," Ruby smiled. "She told me she was going out for dinner with you. Why don't you step inside for a minute? She will be ready soon. I have been hearing some interesting things lately about Eileen."

"Yeah, I guess you may not be the only one," Jeff replied, as he stepped inside the door. He heard movement in the next room. The next thing he saw was Eileen coming out of her room, dressed up in a beautiful light-coloured blouse, a sweater, and matching pants. It was obvious that this evening meant something special for her.

"Are you ready?" Jeff asked.

"Yes, let's go," Eileen spoke with the excitement of a teenage girl.

The place where Jeff had decided to take Eileen was a restaurant on the outskirts of town. It had a quiet ambiance. It was the right place for an evening like this.

After the meal and dessert were finished, Jeff and Eileen sat quietly at the table, enjoying the time together. Eileen looked at Jeff. He returned her look. He knew it was time.

"Eileen, I want to ask you something," He began, and then paused.

"All right," she said, with beaming eyes, "what is it that you want to ask me?"

Jeff pondered for a moment, and then reached into his coat pocket and took out a little box. He slowly opened it, facing Eileen, and looked in her eyes. "Eileen, will you marry me?"

Eileen was surprised, even though she had sort of expected this. "Jeff!" she exclaimed. "Yes, my answer is yes!"

Jeff felt like he was floating on air. He had felt this way once before, when he had asked Faye. But he had not dreamed that, after having lost her, and the four long years of loneliness, that this was a possibility, a second time in one lifetime.

Jeff reached for her hand, and held it to his lips, kissing it. He slid the engagement ring onto her finger and held her hand, looking deeply into her eyes. "I love you, Eileen."

Eileen returned his look, with soft and tender eyes. "And I love you, Jeff."

For a while, neither of them said anything. It was as if they were in a holy place in those moments. Words couldn't do justice to the feelings that were between them.

"Now that we are engaged, we need to decide a wedding date, Jeff," Eileen said, sweetly.

"Well, you are right," Jeff responded. "No point in getting engaged if we are not going to get married, right? When would be good?" Jeff asked.

"How about springtime, perhaps in late May some time?" Eileen suggested.

“May sounds good to me. I just have to make sure I get time off work for a few weeks, to get everything ready,” Jeff responded.

“ ‘We’ have to get everything ready,” Eileen said. “It will be both of us, right?”

“Oh yes, of course. I guess I was not thinking,” Jeff replied. “I have been living alone and doing everything on my own for so long that I have gotten used to it too much. Let’s do some planning in the next while. How does that sound to you?”

“I would like that.” Eileen responded.

They talked on into the evening. It was getting late when they decided to go back. Jeff dropped Eileen off at her place and walked her to the door. He held her for a few moments and placed a light kiss on her lips. “Good night Eileen,” he said, gently. “I will call you during the week.”

That night, when Jeff drove home from Eileen’s apartment, he felt like a king once again. His life was coming around. His ship was free and sailing again, in warmer waters.

Jeff had to work that Saturday, but he didn’t seem to mind. His body was at work, but his mind was with Eileen. Sunday, they would be together in church as an engaged couple.

Chapter 18

The next few months were busy for Jeff and Eileen. With the wedding coming up, there was a lot of work that needed to be done. Jeff knew that, in no time, the wedding day would be here and life would change in a big way for him, again. Jeff began to do some remodelling in the house. He wanted it to be nice for his new wife when she moved in with him.

One of the things that he needed to work through, was the matter with his dogs. He knew Eileen didn't like dogs, and she had not shown any interest in the dogs since he had met her. He was not sure if she would get used to them. So, he had decided that he was not going to make the dogs an issue, even though he liked his dogs very much. They had been his good pets and companions in many of the dark days after Faye had died. But life had changed. He would be getting married. Because his house was small, with only two bedrooms, he could not imagine Eileen liking the dogs or getting used to them. To keep the dogs would keep a link with the past, and it would not help Eileen. He would find out if Mrs. Paten would be interested in taking them, as she had been the one who took them for a daily walk.

One Monday evening, in April, when he came home from work he called Mrs. Paten and told her of his decision regarding the dogs. He asked her if she would be interested in taking them. She responded that she would talk it over with her husband, and, if he agreed, than they would take them. The next evening, she called back saying that her husband was interested, and so they arranged for the dogs to make the transition. Mrs. Paten began taking them home with her and keeping them overnight. Jeff gave the Patens the fence and the kennel he had used for them behind his house. Jeff helped Mr. Paten to put it all up. The dogs adjusted very quickly to their new home.

Eileen insisted that Jeff allow her to help with some of the remodelling work on the house. Jeff had planned on doing it alone, but figured there was no harm in allowing Eileen to help. She seemed to get a lot of satisfaction from working side by side with him.

One evening, as Jeff and Eileen were working, Eileen suddenly noticed something. "What happened to your dogs?"

"I gave them a new home."

"But why did you do that? Don't you like your dogs?"

"Of course, I like my dogs. They are good dogs and have been very good for me. That is why I am giving them away. I would not destroy them. I know your feelings toward dogs, and don't want to put you through that stress, of having to get used to them," Jeff said pleasantly. "They will be well cared for. I offered them to the Pate's down the road, and they are happy to take them. I got everything moved over there, the fence, the kennel ... they will be happy there." Jeff smiled at her from where he was scraping paint from a a door frame.

"Jeff, you never cease to surprise me," Eileen commented. "I had just assumed that getting used to the dogs would be up to me. That was something I had decided not to talk to you about, since I saw how close you were to your animals. I just assumed that they would stay, and I would eventually get used to them."

"You need to remember that you are number one in my life now," Jeff replied. "Everything I do has to be in your best interest first. You need to know that, for me to serve you, I have to watch out for your interest first. I know that we didn't talk about the dogs. My mind was made up some time ago when we got engaged. I decided that I would give the dogs away. I don't want to share you with them."

Eileen looked up at Jeff, and smiled. "Jeff, you truly are a gentleman. I had dreamed of men like you when I was in high school. Now I know they exist. And to think that I have been chosen to be the wife of one ... it's more than I can understand."

Jeff stepped over to her, hugged her close and whispered in her ear. "It really all was orchestrated by someone else, not you or me. We didn't do anything. We just went with what was given to us, and here we are. If you think of me as a true gentleman, just give thanks to God for that. I can't take any credit for it."

Eileen's heart felt light as a butterfly, as she continued working away. She had never dreamed that being in the presence of a man could be so good. Ever since her high school days she had felt used and taken advantage of by men. But this was different. She was learning what it meant to be in love with a real man.

On evenings as they worked together on the house, they enjoyed their time together. As the remodelling progressed, Jeff learned that Eileen had a good taste for country themes and colours. For her, being a city girl all her life, Jeff was surprised at how comfortable and free she felt in the country, at his place, and how energetically she tackled the remodelling work of his little house. The fact that he only had a small place didn't seem to bother her in the least.

Jeff and Eileen continued spending many weeknights working together, to get the little house ready for themselves. For Jeff, life had again become what it had been before. His life was rich and full. He was waiting for the day when he would carry Eileen over the threshold of his little house, as his bride.

By the end of April, the wedding invitations had been made and sent out. It was not just an exciting event for Jeff and Eileen. It seemed that a lot of people in the community looked at Jeff with an attitude of respect.

Ever since the story had aired, of how he had rescued Eileen, there seemed to be a certain amount of admiration toward Jeff from many people. Now the news that Jeff Nolan was getting married to Eileen Benson caused quite a bit of interest. Jeff's co-workers were excited for him as well.

After several weeks of work, Jeff and Eileen were satisfied that the house was adequate. They had done quite a bit of remodelling, and the house was now almost ready. It had taken time and hard work, but it had been good for them as an engaged couple, learning how to work together. Jeff had been surprised by how eagerly Eileen learned to work with wood, and how eagerly she picked up tools and wanted to learn how to use them. She said this was something new to her, different from just doing office work day and day out, and working with people, and customers.

All that was left to do on the house was the painting. Jeff promised Eileen that they would also get some furniture. He wanted to get a new bed, one that was new to them both. This surprised Eileen, but then she realized what Jeff had said before, about this being about both of them, both her and him. He didn't want to have the same bed that he and Faye had had.

He also wanted to get a new set of living room furniture and a dining room set. Eileen had insisted that she was fine with what he had. Jeff told her that it was not so much a matter of it not being adequate. It was more a matter of him starting a new chapter with her, Eileen, as his wife. Anything from the past, he wanted to remove for both their sakes. Jeff realized that, not only was his life-ship in warmer waters now, gone from the cold, icy dark wilderness of loneliness and despair, his ship had been given new sails and new paint.

Chapter 19

The wedding day was on a Saturday, at the end of May, and it was clear, warm and sunny. Jeff was up early that day. He had taken off work for that day, and two weeks following that to go on a honey moon with his new bride. Today, he was getting married.

The wedding would be held in the small Hope Fellowship Church. It was in this church that Jeff had married Faye Williamson, more than fourteen years earlier. As much as he had enjoyed that time of his life, that chapter was now closed. He realized that, as wonderful as those years were, and as difficult as the loss of Faye had been, the experience of that time had matured him in his heart.

Today, he was taking Eileen Benson as his wife. He was very aware that life was fragile and could be over in short while. He would simply thank God for the blessings he had been given, and trust that God would see him through anything, as he had during the previous years of his life. He was going to live in the moment, and nothing would be allowed to destroy that moment.

The morning, for him, went by as if in a dream. His house looked very different now from that Saturday morning the previous November, when he had left it to go on that hunting trip and had rescued Eileen. Things had changed so much in such a short time. He found it interesting that he didn't miss his dogs. If someone had wanted him to part with them back then, he would not have been able to let go of them. Now everything was different.

Jeff and Eileen had decided to have a simple wedding, without much of the usual stuff that is done at weddings. They had decided, instead, to spend their money on their honeymoon and enjoy themselves. After all, this was their wedding. They were marrying each other, and not trying to impress the community with a lavish event.

As a wedding gift, his co-workers had pooled their money and rented a late model luxury car, for him to take his bride on their honeymoon. They had figured Jeff's old dodge pickup was not the ideal transportation for a bride. Jeff accepted the gift thankfully and good-naturedly. Even as a Christian, he had the respect and admiration of most of his coworkers, and it showed. Jeff had not expected this kind of generosity from them.

While driving to the church with the rental car, in his mind he went back over the last few months since he had been engaged to Eileen. He and Eileen had met a few times with Pastor Raymond, and had some sessions together with him regarding their upcoming wedding. Pastor Raymond had been very helpful in answering some questions that Eileen had since this was her first marriage, and for Jeff, given his experience with the loss of a previous partner. Both Jeff and Eileen, given their life experiences, and the times they had been through, were under no illusion that life could never be difficult and painful. As Jeff pondered these things, the realization hit him, that the blessings and pleasures of life were meaningful and effective in direct proportion to the potential of pain and loss. If loss and pain were not a possibility, there would not be much value in what they had. He knew from experience that the deepest pain comes from the deepest love. He also realized that he was exposing himself again to the possibility of going through deep pain again. When he thought of what he had felt when he had lost Faye, he realized that, no matter how risky this step in his life was, he would rather die than not experience it. The experience of love was too wonderful, too deep and too powerful not to embrace. He knew people were made to love, and for love.

As he pulled into the driveway of the church, he noticed that Eileen's little Focus was already there, and Eileen was inside. It was only a matter of minutes now.

At two o'clock, Pastor Raymond and Jeff walked into the church. The place was simply, but attractively, decorated. As Pastor Raymond and Jeff walked onto the small stage, and turned to face the audience, Jeff's mind drifted to Eileen. "I wonder what is going through her mind," he thought. He was waiting to see her. The pastor's wife, and a few of the church ladies, had agreed to help her with her preparations. For Eileen, this was still fairly new. She had never experienced community like this. As Jeff stood there, deep in thought, he saw Eileen come into the entrance way of the church. She was stunningly beautiful, in her flowing white dress and veil. It made his heart rate increase, and he smiled at her as she walked into the church. The congregation rose to their feet, as the music played. Jeff watched her come up the aisle slowly, and purposefully. She was coming to the front of the church to become his wife, and he was going to become her husband. It was all in slow motion to him.

The wedding ceremony was short but meaningful. In his devotional, Pastor Raymond commented on the fact that this wedding was special in that this couple, Eileen Benson and Jeff Nolan had met in the strangest of circumstances. Jeff and Eileen had given him permission to use their life's experience as a backdrop for his speech.

Pastor Raymond drew a parallel in Jeff and Eileen's relationship with the story of Christ in the New Testament. "When Jesus saved his bride, which today is the church, it cost him his life. When Jeff rescued Eileen out of danger, he literally put his life on the line. He knew that he was, very possibly, not going to survive that risky undertaking. But what drove him to rescue her is the same thing that drives Christ. It is love. For Jeff and Eileen, this is a special day where they are joining their lives in marriage as an expression of commitment and devotion to each other for a life-long relationship."

After Pastor Raymond had pronounced them husband and wife, Jeff and Eileen exited the building. They would go to take some pictures at a park. and be back for a reception in a few hours. Eileen had hired a photographer from Forest Hill. After the photo session in the park, Jeff and Eileen returned to the church for a reception. From the group of guests, a tidy sum of money was collected, and given to Jeff and Eileen to enjoy themselves with on their honeymoon.

Jeff and Eileen opened the presents their friends and coworkers had given them. They found some gift cards, some cards with money, but the most special card for Jeff was the card from Pastor Raymond. It read: "Jeff, you are an image of what it looks like when God works in a human being. Congratulations to both of you on your marriage. Eileen, you married a real gentleman."

After the gifts were put back in boxes, Jeff and Eileen put them in the rental car and headed back to Jeff's house. Eileen had asked Ruby Miller if she would take her Ford Focus home with her, where they would pick it up after the honeymoon.

When Jeff and Eileen arrived at Jeff's place, to pick up the suitcases for their trip, Jeff walked Eileen up to the door and stepped forward to unlock it. He opened it, turned to Eileen, picked her up in his strong arms, and carried her over the threshold. Eileen felt as if she floated on air. He looked her in the eyes, kissed her, and set her on her feet.

"Jeff," she said. "This is the most glorious day of my life. I feel like life has just started. Even if we didn't go on a honeymoon, I could not be happier."

Jeff laughed. "We are going on a honeymoon, dear, we have reserved our nights and we will enjoy them."

"I know, Jeff. It's just that I never knew that being in love with a gentleman could be so good!"

Jeff responded with a laughing smile. "You make me happy saying that, Eileen. Our marriage ship has set sail. We are ready, let's go." He kissed his bride and felt the wind in his soul as his heart set sail with his wife on a new journey.

Acknowledgments:

I am indebted to my loving Wife Anna, my sons, my wider family and many dear friends who encouraged and supported me in my decision to put my thoughts to print.

I also am indebted to the staff at Friesen Press for their advice, support and guidance in helping me publish this book